Ablutions

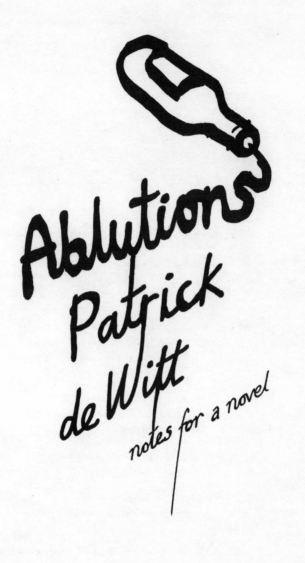

Ablutions

Patrick
de Witt

notes for a novel

GRANTA

Granta Publications, 12 Addison Avenue, London W11 4QR

First published in Great Britain by Granta Books, 2009
First published in the United States by
Houghton Mifflin Harcourt, 2009

A portion of this book previously appeared, in different form,
in *Userlands: New Fiction from the Blogging Underground*.

A CIP catalogue record for this book
is available from the British Library.

1 3 5 7 9 10 8 6 4 2

ISBN 978 1 84708 095 0

Printed and bound in the UK by
CPI William Clowes, Beccles NR34 7TL

*For my father, Gary deWitt*
*the last of the old, bold pilots*

# One

DISCUSS THE REGULARS. They sit in a line like ugly, huddled birds, eyes wet with alcohol. They whisper into their cups and seem to be gloating about something—you will never know what. Some have jobs, children, spouses, cars, and mortgages, while others live with their parents or in transient motels and are on government assistance, a curious balance of classes particular to the parts of Hollywood devoid of klieg lights and make-believe. There are sometimes limousines at the curb out front; other nights feature police cars and ambulances and vicious street scenarios. The bar interior resembles a sunken luxury liner of the early 1900s, mahogany and brass, black-burgundy leather coated in dust and ash. It is impossible to know how many times the ownership has changed hands.

The regulars are warm with one another but generally come and go alone and as far as you can tell have never been to one another's homes. This makes you lonely and the hearts of the world seem cold and stingy and you are reminded of the saying, every man for himself, which as a child made you want to lie down and "be killed."

You do not take much stock in the North American definition of the word but you suppose these people are alcoholics. They like you, or anyway are used to you, and they reach out to touch you when you pass as though you are a good-luck gambling charm. You once found this repulsive and would circle the bar with your back hugging the wall rather than move through the network of fleshy red hands, but you have reconciled yourself to the attention and it has become familiar, even enjoyable for you. It now feels more like a commendation than an intrusion, recognition of your difficult job, and you nod and smile as the hands grab you around the waist, rubbing and slapping your back and belly.

From your post at the side bar entrance you watch them watch themselves in the mirror behind the bar. Preening, pecking, satisfied by their reflections—what do they see in their murky silhouettes? You wonder keenly about their lives prior to their residence here. Strange as it seems, they must have been regulars at some other Hollywood bar, but had moved on or been asked to move on, and they sought out a new retreat, settling down with the first free beer or kind word, some bartender's impotent joke mutilated beyond recognition in its endless retelling. And the regulars turned to tell the joke once more.

You wonder also about their present lives but to make inquiries is purposeless—the regulars are all sensational liars. But you want to know what it is about their existence that fuels the need to inhabit not just the same building every night but the same barstool, upon which they sip the same drink. And if a bartender forgets a regular's usual, the regular is cut down and his eyes swell with a lost suffering. Why? It bothers you to know that the truth will never reveal itself spontaneously and you keep on your toes for clues.

WHEN YOU FIRST COME to work at the bar you drink Claymore, the least expensive or what is called the well scotch. This was your brand when you were out in the world and you are happy to finally find a never-ending, complimentary supply. You have been at the bar for two years, drinking Claymore in great quantity, sometimes straight, oftentimes with ginger ale or cola, before the manager, Simon, asks why you don't drink the quality liquors. "There aren't many upsides to the life, but I drink the best booze," he says. And so each night you sample a different scotch or whiskey. There are more than forty-five different types of scotch and whiskey and you are very tired at the end of your quest but you find at long last the quality liquor Simon spoke of. As someone who spends a good deal of time surrounded by alcohol, people often ask what you drink, and now you do not shrug or cough but look up and say directly, "I drink John Jameson finest Irish whiskey."

YOU FALL IN LOVE with Jameson Irish whiskey. Previously when you held a bottle of alcohol in your hands you felt a comfort in knowing that its contents would simultaneously deaden and heighten your limited view of the world but you did not care for the actual bottle, as you do now with Jameson, you did not trace your hands over the raised lettering and study the exquisite script. One night you are alone in the back bar doing just this—the bottle is in your hands and you are mooning over the curlicues at the base of the label—and the name John Jameson brings into your head the child's tune "John Jacob Jingleheimer Schmidt." You are humming this to yourself when Simon, the man responsible for your discovery of Jameson whiskey, enters the bar singing aloud *this very same song*. He waves to you and walks past, into the front bar, and you are staring in disbelief because there is no explaining so obscure a coincidence and you feel you have been visited by the strongest of omens. Good or bad, you do not know. There is nothing to do but wait and see.

Now a group of drunks up front have picked up the song and are singing in the single voice of a runaway giant.

Discuss the ghost woman that hovers beside the tequila bottles. Like all murdered ghosts she is in need of impossible assistance. There is a mirror running the length of the bar and as you set up for business you see or believe you see furtive movements of light just over your shoulder and in the reflection of your eyeglasses. This happens hundreds of times, so you come to take it for granted when, one night, alone in the bar, the ghost stops you in your tracks with a cold weight-force centered at your shoulder. You feel as though all the air has been pulled from your lungs and mouth and you cannot breathe in or out and you push forward again and this time do not feel the terrible force but the tequila bottles rattle as you move past. You cannot leave the bar unattended and no one will arrive to assist you for over an hour and what you really need is a nice big drink of Jameson but you cannot bring yourself to walk past the tequilas to the whiskey assortment. If you ever hear the rattling again, you say to yourself, you will drop your head on the metal sink edge and knock yourself out, and you see in your mind the image of your unconscious body sprawled on the rubber mats behind the bar. The ghost is fully formed and hanging over as if to injure you but your lights are out and nobody's home and so the ghost, dissolving, returns wanly to the tequila.

You HAVE BAD TEETH and your breath is poor. Your tips consequently are also poor and there is clotted blood in your mouth and you lose tooth pieces on soft foods like mashed potatoes and rice. You are talking to the bar owner's wife when an entire molar comes dislodged and lies heavily on your tongue. You hope to keep the tooth a secret but you are speaking strangely and her head is cocked in wonder. You have begun to sweat and blush and you pray that she does not ask what the problem is but she is opening her mouth and this is just what she does. You swallow the molar and hold out your palms to show that you are not hiding anything. You are an honest man with a clean, hopeful heart.

Discuss THE NEW doorman, Antony, who at the end of his third night on the job accidentally cuts a man's thumb off. Antony is a talented mixed martial artist known for first-round knockouts and an apparent inability to feel pain. He is bitter that he has to pick up bar shifts to survive and he wonders if his management team is skimming more than what is customary. You find him intriguing and are impressed with his prejudice when he tells you he listens exclusively to West Coast hip-hop. Anything written or produced outside of California is of no interest to him; there are no exceptions to this rule. Antony takes a shine to you because you are so skinny and white. He is Puerto Rican and wonders at your drunken life. He asks if you eat only one Cheeto per day and you tell him that sometimes if you are famished you will eat two. You tell him you are available as a sparring partner on Tuesdays and Sundays.

The lights are up and Antony is shouting for everyone to leave the bar. He is learning that people want more than anything not to leave and will have many excuses at the ready, but now their excuses are running thin and his mood is ugly. He has kicked everyone out and moves to close the heavy steel door when Simon calls out his name and he turns. He speaks with Simon while trying to close the door but it is jammed and he slams the door three times with all his weight and finally the latch catches and he walks away but hears a wailing outside and returns to look out the peephole and there is the man with the missing thumb spinning around and bleeding and Antony is stepping on something, later he says he thought it was an old cigar. The thumb is cleaned and wrapped in ice and given to a friend of the man who lost it and they rush off to the hospital together, and you tease Antony, calling him a terrific racist intent on de-fingering innocent white men. His eyes rise level to yours and you see that he is heartbroken by what he has done. "I know how important a man's hands are," he says. His shoulders are trembling and the bar workers say nothing. It is at this moment that you fall platonically in love with Antony.

WHEN YOU SLEEP, your dreams are those of a dullard: You polish ashtrays, stock the ice bins, reach for a bottle and find it there or not there, and exchange names and pleasantries with familiar-looking customers. These scenarios run in a spinning wheel and are identical in texture to your drunken memories. As a result you have only a dim idea what is fact and what is fiction and are constantly referencing past conversations with people you have never spoken with or else ignoring those you had for fear you had not. And so the general public is of split minds about you: Some say you are stupid, and some say you are rude.

Discuss the ingesting of pills in the storage room at seven o'clock and waiting on a barstool for the high to hit. There is a faint chalk line of daylight at the base of the front door and two customers are looking over at you. Their drinks are empty and they want to call out but you make them uncomfortable. Why, they are wondering, is that man smiling? The bar is silent and the pills congregate in your fingertips like lazy students in an empty hall.

Discuss the effects of the full moon on the weekend crowds and the dread you experience when you see the full moon wedged in the corner of the sky. Discuss the short muscleman who is stripped to the waist and eager to fight. He hits a larger man over the head with a bottle and is apprehended by a doorman. The muscleman makes a show of taking his time to leave and so when he reaches the exit there are many angry people waiting for him on the sidewalk. You move to the door to watch because the world is full of short musclemen wanting to fight and you hope to see one hurt or killed.

The muscleman stands behind two doormen and spouts profane threats to the people on the sidewalk; the man with the head wound stands at the front of the pack, proud of his bloody face. His injury has awakened a subtle greatness in him and he licks at the blood and his eyes are wild and wonderful and it is just as he says: He is going to murder the muscleman. The doormen are in no danger but do not like protecting a villain and finally they give up the muscleman to be slaughtered when he will not keep his mouth closed. He is backed against the building and to the last is confident he will emerge victorious and he asks the crowd of twenty who will be first and there comes an answer in the form of a tremendous fist in his face. The fist belongs to the man with the head wound, who is delighted with the punch, as well he should be—it is as in a heroic dream. The muscleman drops like a stone and the crowd swarms over him in search of available openings.

DISCUSS CURTIS, a disconsolate black man and regular with a law enforcement fetish. He wears a bulky leather motorcycle-cop jacket and mirrored cop sunglasses and a heavy leather gun holster without a gun in it. He has another holster on his belt for his Zippo lighter; he knows many tricks involving the lighter and offers people cigarettes so that he might showcase them, though Curtis himself does not smoke. He suffers from the skin condition vitiligo and both his hands from the knuckles to the fingertips are patchy with raw, pink flesh. He plays the Rolling Stones' "Memory Hotel" over and over on the jukebox, a song you once liked but which he has poisoned for you. He sings along, eager to show that he knows every word, and his tongue falls from his mouth like a tentacle, his gums like dirty purple curtains. His hair is short, with a part shaved into the side of his head; he has a silver-dollar-sized bald spot to which he applies an egg-smelling cream, the scent of which oftentimes alerts you to his presence. His head bobs deeply as he drinks and his neck stretches long like caramel taffy on a pull.

He has many annoying habits, not the least of which is mimicking your brand of drink. When you made the final switch to Jameson, for instance, Curtis followed suit. When your liver began to ache and you took to mixing ginger ale into your whiskey and chasing this with cranberry juice, Curtis did as well. This could be the sincerest form of flattery but most likely it is his plan to instill in your subconscious the repellent notion that you and he are kindred spirits. Also this practice of copycatting makes it easy for him to shout out that you should make it two when he sees you moving toward the bottles to fix yourself something. After the drink slips down his throat he bombards you with praise and brays at any little joke you make, though it cannot be said that he is looking for friendship, only free whiskey. You supply him with this because he has been drinking on the house for years and the alternative would be to sit him down and essentially break up with him, and because the whiskey after all is not yours, and it is easier to give it away than to have so intimate a conversation with someone you spend every night trying your best to avoid even glancing at.

Curtis was not always like this. When he first came around he was a model customer. He tipped well and bought rounds and picked up tabs that were not his and at the end of each night he would help clean the bar or stock beer and was bashful and sweet if you should thank him. He never got overly drunk, he never leered at women, he rarely spoke and then never about himself, and he never once wore his mirrored sunglasses indoors. Everyone liked him, you included, and you showered him with warmth and gratitude, and eventually with alcohol.

He had at first refused any complimentary drinks, feigning shock, as though the idea was the farthest thing from his mind. Then he allowed it infrequently, and only when it was demanded of him, and his tips would reflect his appreciation of the gesture. Slowly, though, he accepted the drinks more and more and in time, six months perhaps, it was understood that Curtis was one of those who drank on the house. Once this was established, once he was inextricably enmeshed in the fiber of the bar, once he became a *regular,* then he began to change, or as you believe, to reveal his true self, the man he had been all along: He took an interest in women and became one of those who approached and bothered them; he drank to the point of drunkenness and spoke of his life, or rather, lied about his life, and the lies were feeble articles, too sad even to handle and dismantle; he ceased helping with the after-hours chores but stayed on all the same, making asides and offering peppy talks where none were needed; and finally his tips trickled away, from tens to fives to ones to change to nothing at all, and this was the worst aspect of the new Curtis because he hoped to replace the divot in the tip jar with his oppressive, counterfeit friendship. Now he stares long and hard until you cannot help but return his gaze, and he motions you over as if you were close companions with great things to share. He imparts an obvious falsehood about an imaginary girlfriend before squeezing your shoulder and asking if you have had a drink lately, and if you tell him you have not he says, let's the both of us have one together. If you say that you have he tells you to slow it down until he catches up and he asks with reptilian humility for a double shot of whiskey and a beer, anything cold, anything besides Budweiser, or Pabst, or Tecate, and he names off all the beers besides Guinness, the most expensive beer, which is what he wanted all along.

It has been so long since Curtis was the model customer

that most do not remember the phase at all, or else they say that he tipped and was helpful on only one rare day. Those who do remember assume Curtis has fallen on hard times and take pity on him, but you know he has a job in a Kinko's copy shop because you have driven by and seen him at work. He could still tip but chooses not to, and you believe he has studied each bar employee and decided that there is not one in the bunch who cares enough about his or her job to put a stop to his endless tab, and in this he is correct. You sometimes see this knowledge glowing in his eyes, and see how badly he wants to share it with someone, anyone, but he doesn't dare for fear this will affect his tenuous standing, and each time he receives a drink he is greatly relieved and he laughs aloud and thinks to himself, How much longer will these people let me drink for free?

One night he is drunk and whispering into the ear of an unaccompanied woman. You cannot tell what he is saying and you do not want to know but the woman is offended and you see her jerk back and douse him with her drink and she calls Curtis a loser and his ridiculous, agonized expression somehow crystallizes the word's definition and you are traumatized to finally understand its true meaning—that is, someone who has lost, and who is losing, and who will continue to lose for the rest of his life until he is dead and in the ground. She leaves the bar and Curtis retires to the bathroom to dry his face and holsters. He returns as though nothing has happened, and before he can begin telepathically attacking you, you head for the bottle of Jameson and pour out two large shots. Curtis wants to drink to friendship but you opt for health, and he shrugs and pours the whiskey down his throat and you see his tonsils glistening as he tips back the glass to drain it.

By last call his face is on the bar and his bald spot is slick and beaming under the lights and you feel a warmth toward him because there is something childlike about his head and skull, something innocent and fine, and you worry for the skull, propped and dozing, and you think to wrap it in cotton and set it in a cupboard for safekeeping, but when he raises his red eyes to meet yours, whatever tenderness you had for him trickles away and is gone. Now you hate him and you tell him he has to go home and he turns to the glowing green EXIT sign that hangs above the door. Following its instruction he moves out and into the night, staggering as he goes. "See you tomorrow," he calls back, and you set your teeth to grinding. The sinks are full with cold brown water and your arm is like a hook as you dump in all the dirty glasses and you hear the muted sound of glass breaking underwater and want to plunge your palms in and shred them through but you only empty the sinks and watch the mound of glass shards shining under the lurid red light of the bar.

YOU LIKE TO THINK that if you were ever attacked by a shark you would afterward swim in the ocean without the slightest fear because statistically it would be impossible to be attacked again. This is your feeling on the subject of the ghost: Your quota of naked terror is now full and you will not be bothered anymore. You no longer see her in the mirrors or hear the rattling of bottles and you tell yourself that the weight-force on your shoulder was only fantasy, another of your bar dreams. And yet you still think of her, and from time to time engage her or the idea of her in conversation, asking questions like, "How do you think tonight will go for me?" and "What do the bosses say about me when I'm not around?" as well as "Are you cold?" and "Do you carry the woes of the world on your very shoulders?" and also, once, "Do you see how differently the young women dress today?" A voice resides in your head to answer these and other questions. It is a wise and sexless voice and you cultivate its sound and are happy to have created so fine a being, but the voice sometimes frightens you, as it seems to know things you do not. For instance, you are often poked and stabbed with broken glasses and bottles and your hands are marked with many small cuts. You invent a game where you run your hands under hot water and with eyes closed attempt to pinpoint and count them, but the pain makes the wounds blur into one another and when you open your eyes to check you have always missed a cut or two or added a cut or two, and you laugh at the silly diversion.

One night, after hours, you are alone and running your hands under the hot water when the voice asks if you aren't through with your ablutions yet. You do not know the word but write it down to look it up the next day. You learn its definition on page 3 of *Merriam-Webster's Collegiate Dictionary:* "The washing of one's body or part of it (as in a religious rite)." You are certain you have never heard this word before as you were raised without any religion and have never set foot inside any church or temple, and you return the dictionary to the shelf and vow never to play this game of counting your wounds again.

YOU DRIVE HOME DRUNK at the end of each night but the police have never stopped you because your car, a 1971 Ford LTD, is magical. It is a twenty-minute drive through empty streets and highways from the bar to your home and by rights you should have been arrested a hundred times over, but the car's powers are such that even when police drive behind you they are rendered blind and deaf to your weaving and your squealing tires. You sometimes do not remember driving home at all and later find dents and scratches in the front and back fenders, but each morning you awake in your bed and not in a jail cell and you wonder if the car became magical only after you owned it or if it rolled off the assembly line this way.

You believe the Ford's magic is ever growing like money in the bank, like a slow-blossoming flower, but you have had the car since you were sixteen years old and so despite its powers you do not want to drive it or look upon its decrepit exterior anymore and you retire it to the carport where it becomes host to an unfriendly stray tomcat and a variety of spiders whose many webs embroider the interior like a lace doily. You place a newspaper ad in hopes of selling the car but no one will purchase a vehicle in such a state: The convertible top is permanently down, the plates are out of state, the steering wheel has a quarter turn of slack, the doors do not open, the right rear wheel wobbles, the seats are shredded, the radio turns on and off at will, and the gas pedal sticks when you drop it to the floor. You tell potential buyers about the car's crafty, police-eluding talents, but they only point to the rust and the broken taillights and walk away thinking of their wasted time. Eventually you give up on the idea of selling the car and begin taking your wife's Toyota to work.

The Toyota is not magical and it seems that each time you drink and drive there is a policeman lurking in the rear-view mirror. Whenever this happens you decide that if you are pulled over you will tell the policeman directly that you are drunk and ask to be jailed at once, but the red and blue lights somehow never come on and the police car rushes past you toward some fatal danger or another. Your hands tremble and you turn down a side street to park and you think of the repercussions of a DUI and swear never to drink and drive again and all the next day you feel righteous and masterful but that night you misplace your purpose and drink and drive again. It makes you sad that you can't keep a promise to yourself but you are of two minds on the matter. The minds are cleanly separated and functioning independently of each other. They are content with this arrangement and have no plans to alter it.

Your luck is buckling. Someone gives you a handful of pills that you eat along with your nightly whiskey and as the narcotics take effect a love grows in your heart and you wonder if this isn't how saints feel. But you are drinking more and more and the feeling is hidden in ugly clouds and by night's end you are unable to speak and you walk to the gas station to purchase aspirin. You are slurring your words and the Arab man behind the bulletproof glass does not like you. Now he is standing over you and shaking you awake: You have fallen asleep in the gas station bathroom, though you do not know why you entered or how long you have been there. You return to your car and find a note on the windshield: "Where did you go?" The note is not signed and the love in your heart is gone. It feels as if it was never there at all.

You are driving. A car is approaching in your lane and it seems you will collide with it. Both cars' brakes lock up but there is a slight accident. You pull over and a man jumps from the other car looking to attack you physically. It was not he in the wrong lane but you and his front fender is dented and he is furious. He is all muscle and it appears you will be beaten for your careless driving. Your blood is a dead weight in your veins and you are very confused by what has happened and the man asks if you are drunk and you say that you never drink, not even wine on Sundays, as you are devoutly religious and believe that alcohol is the handiwork of the devil himself. You manage to say this without a stutter and the man stands back to look at you. His anger is diffused by your proclamation and now he is searching high and low for it. If he could only reclaim the anger he would carry on with his original plan, which was to hurt you as you hurt his automobile, but now a policeman has pulled over a drunk across the street and the man's demeanor changes. You know by the look in his eyes that he is afraid of the police and you decide he must have a warrant, or else he is drunk himself or has drugs in his car or on his person. The man says again that he suspects you have been drinking, and pointing to the policeman he asks what you would say to a field sobriety test. Knowing the man is bluffing you say that would be fine and you clear your throat to shout out to the policeman when the man lays a hand on your arm to silence you. He writes out your address and license plate number and he is cursing but his anger is gone and will not come back.

The drunk across the street is in the back of the police car and the policeman is watching you. He is curious and it seems he will cross the street to meet you and you tell the man into whom you crashed about this and he is scared. "Let's pretend we're good friends saying goodnight to each other," you say, and you take up the man's hand to shake it. "Okay!" you say. This is what you imagine one good friend would say to another at three o'clock in the morning on the side of the road in Hollywood. "Okay!" you say again. "Okay!" the man says. He is crushing your hand and you are smiling. "I still think you're drunk," he whispers. You wink and return to the Toyota. The policeman has lost interest and is filling out paperwork on his dashboard; the drunk is watching you from the back of the squad car. You point to him and tip back a phantom bottle, and he nods. He points to you and tips a phantom bottle and you nod. The drunk then points skyward, toward heaven, and to his heart. This is a beautiful gesture from a man on his way to jail and as you pull back onto the road you decide to have a cry over it. You try to cry all the way home but can manage only a coughing fit and a few moans. You had hoped your crying would be so relentless that you would be forced to pull the car over and "ride it out," but you arrive home without shedding a tear. You fall asleep in the Toyota and when you wake up you are covered with sweat and your wife is hitting you and shrieking in what seems to be another language and you say to her, "Okay! Okay! Okay!" She is curious about the damage done to the front of the car and her sharpened red fingers stab crazily at the morning air.

CURTIS LOSES HIS JOB and begins bringing things from his apartment into the bar as tips: Stereo equipment, DVDs, a video camera, and compact discs. At first the gifts are wrapped and labeled for individual employees but as his possessions dwindle he begins filling a gym bag with whatever detritus is lying around his room—books mostly, mutilated, frantically highlighted texts offering too clear a glimpse into Curtis's private life: *An Illustrated History of S&M, Grappling for Dummies, Homemade Explosives 1-2-3.* When there is nothing left to give, Curtis stuffs his coat pockets with pornographic magazines and hands these out indiscriminately throughout the night, speaking all the while of friendship and lasting cheer and the importance of sticking together. You now bring him drinks if only to condense your conversations and divert his increasingly psychotic gaze. No one else seems to notice his decline, but you expect he will shortly crack and run rampant with a knife, or lob a pipe bomb into the bar. It will sever your body at the waist and your legs will cancan out the door, heading west toward the ocean on Santa Monica Boulevard.

Curtis is waiting by the Toyota after hours. He wants a ride home. You are drunk and cannot think of a lie to tell him and you walk around to unlock his door as if you were on a date. You are driving along in silence when he begins, out of the blue, to weep on your shoulder. You do not know what to do. You want to crash into a wall and die. He is also drunk and talking through a bubbling mask of spittle; now he will tell you his story. He has been evicted, he says, but breaks into the apartment to sleep sitting up in the closet. The new tenants are due at any moment and he lives in unending fear of their arrival and hasn't slept more than three hours a night for the past week and what little sleep he has had was riddled with nightmares. (He is standing by the sea watching two large red fish casually eating each other's faces. Soon they are but two wagging, blood-spitting tails.) You extend your sympathies but feel in your heart that Curtis has found his station in life, that he *belongs* in a closet dreaming of murderous sea life, that he *deserves* to live in a state of perpetual unease. And yet it is an awful fate, and you place a pitying hand on his shoulder and tell him that everything will work itself out.

"When?" he asks.

You are idling in front of Curtis's/not Curtis's apartment and he leans in gripping your hand and asks with absolute earnestness if he might live with you and your wife. He cannot pay you any rent but is handy with around-the-house repairs and will be happy to run errands. He says it will take him three to five months to get back on his feet and through the murk and fog of your drunken mind you are visited by the image of Curtis in his underwear sitting on the couch in

20

your living room shouting at the television set. This fills you with hysterical apprehension and your ensuing fit of laughter is completely out of your control. Now Curtis is gloomy and will not get out of the car. He asks for five dollars and you give him twenty and it occurs to you that you are witnessing the birth of a homeless man, and you will never again be one of those who look upon a staggering wino and say, "How did he get to be so low down?" Curtis is muttering bitterly from the passenger seat; he seems almost to be mimicking the idling engine. *Putter putter putter*—it has been a long Saturday night and you are tired and the sound lulls you to sleep and when you wake up at dawn you are alone and the car has run itself out of gas.

DISCUSS THE APARTMENT building across from the bar. It sits above a massage parlor and twice you see people drop from a high window to the sidewalk. You do not cross the street to view the results but your heart is hurt and confused by the sight of the falling bodies. They fall with certainty or with confidence; they seem to want to fall faster. (In your dreams, the bodies are always falling and will always fall from this building. You are always standing on the sidewalk, smoking and staring at their point of departure.)

You do not ask about but overhear the doormen speak of the incidents and you learn that the first was a suicide, the second a homicide. A third falling body follows on a night you are off sick and you feel as though you have missed an important engagement. Tony, the man who collects the empty bottles at closing time, sits with a beer listening to the after-hours talk of the building and bodies and he leans in and tells you it is the building's will to expel its occupants. With a fluttering, arcing hand he says, "The Terrible Building That Vomits Humans."

Discuss simon, the managing bartender. He was born and raised in Johannesburg, South Africa; after winning a modeling competition he immigrated to Hollywood at twenty years of age. Now forty, his hair is still white-blond and full, his body still fit and tanned, but after two decades of alcohol and cocaine abuse his face is beginning to sag, his dreams of success as an actor growing increasingly irrelevant. He swivels at the hips like an action-figure doll and delivers clipped witticisms and superfluous personal information with shocking redundancy. If, for instance, he has decided once more to quit drinking he will be sure to tell every customer about it all through the night, whether they are interested or not. "It's a question of mind over matter, mate," he will say. A few days later he will tell the same people about his plan to abstain for three long months. He is "Givin' the liver a breather, buddy." A week later he will be back to drinking tequila and when confronted with his earlier proclamations will plead ignorance or say that he had only been joking. He is the type who drops his towel in the sauna so that if you look—you cannot help but look—you will see his chiseled buttocks and uncircumcised penis, an image that will flash in your mind's eye for days to come like a death threat.

As manager, Simon has the unpleasant job of keeping the employees in line, and you sometimes find that he is screaming at you. He screams only when you are very drunk and so the gravity of his reproach is always misplaced and forgotten and the next day at work he will apologize and you will not know what he is talking about but you will forgive him anyway and he will bring over two drinks so that you might restore peace and you will empty the glass and think, This must be how it feels to have a stepfather.

E ACH MORNING YOU WAKE up wondering how hung-over you will be. You are partially asleep or partially drunk or both and at first you cannot gauge your own suffering and you cast a hand outward and ask yourself, how does this hand feel? What about the arm, the shoulder, the chest, the torso? Is there any aching or discomfort in the legs? On a pain scale of one to ten (one is a finger-flick to your skull, ten is death), what is the rating from the neck up? You blink your eyes to test their sensitivity to light and crane your neck to crack your spine and gravity is pushing on your swollen, dehydrated brain and you inspect your body for wounds or tenderness. You are your own doctor, sympathetic but ultimately disconnected.

Your wife enters the room and you sit up in bed to greet her, a sudden movement revealing that you have a spectacular hangover and are in considerable pain. Your body is humming and your blood seems to be running against itself and you can hear your blood churning and try to describe this sound to yourself: A toy engine submerged in water. A propeller plane buzzing in the sky. The plane is hidden in fog. It is ten miles off.

Your wife is folding and unfolding sheets. She asks how you are feeling and you say the word *great*. She says you seemed drunk the night before, that you were singing, and you tell her you were not drunk but jolly. She heard you fall in the bathroom, she says, and you claim to have slipped on a sock. It was not your sock but hers and you could have been knocked unconscious. You could have been killed. Your wife says nothing to this but sighs, and you tell her that if she still doesn't believe you then to go ahead and count out the aspirin in the bathroom cupboard (she always counts out the aspirin in the bathroom cupboard), for if you had been drunk, as she says, you would surely have eaten some before bedtime. Count out the aspirin, you say again, and see that none are missing, but she does not budge, she only nods, and you know by the somberness of the gesture that she has already found the aspirin all accounted for. She moves to the kitchen to make herself a cup of tea and there is a resonant crash as she drops the kettle into the sink to fill it and you wince at the sound and flip your pillow in hopes that the cooler cotton will chill your whiskey-warm face.

Your wife has long suspected you of covertly purchasing and consuming aspirin on your way home from work and she rifles the car for empty Advil packets and telltale 7-Eleven receipts. In these investigations she is always unsuccessful, as you are careful to discard your aspirin evidence, but she is certain that at some point each night you are floating aspirin atop a bellyful of whiskey and doing your body irreparable damage that will shorten your time together. She has cried about your aspirin abuse and once cursed you and demanded to know your aspirin secrets, but you only held her and told her lies. (She knew you were telling her lies.) What she does not know is that you have a bottle of aspirin tucked in the back of your study closet and that you eat them like strongman vitamins. What she does not know is that at another time, in another neighborhood, and hidden from another woman, you kept aspirin in the glove compartment of your magical car. Once you hid your aspirin in a shoebox, once in an acoustic guitar. You have always hidden your aspirin from some nosy woman who thought to come to the aid of your defenseless organs. When the woman went away you would move your aspirin into your bathroom cupboard and gobble them freely and without fear of reprimand, but sooner or later a new woman would arrive and declare your lifestyle unhealthy and you would be forced once more to hide the bottle. This routine only brings you closer to your aspirin and you come to adore them in a star-crossed-lovers type of way. It is a doomed affair and will end in misery and death.

Now your wife's kettle is boiling (she is punishing you by letting its whistle blow) and there is apricot-colored bile rising from your stomach like mercury in a thermometer. If your wife finds you vomiting there will be no debating whether or not you are hung-over and your plans for the day will be ruined. (In the nighttime you dreamt of a cold movie palace and its rippling red curtain rising to reveal distraction from the coming day's agony.) You get out of bed sweating your whiskey sweat and your head is dizzy and pulsing and you are walking in the agitated hunchback style, first to your study for the aspirin and then to the bathroom, where you turn on the shower and radio and drop to your knees before the toilet.

You are a trained silent vomiter. You do not sigh, you do not moan, you do not breathe heavily, you vomit on the porcelain of the toilet rather than in the toilet water, and as far as your wife knows you have never once vomited in all your time together. This skill was not developed overnight and you are annoyed that you will never be able to share it with others, and you wonder if you wouldn't benefit from having a best friend. But wouldn't he then want to share his talents with you? And is this perhaps all that best friends do? Sit around discussing their talents? You are not interested in the talents of others and you decide you must be cautious about whom you let into your life.

You flush the toilet and watch your vomit as though it is a

departing train. Your stomach is empty and you will probably not vomit again on this day and you decide to take five aspirin, this in addition to the six you took the night before for a total of eleven in eight hours, which according to aspirin labels, doctors, girlfriends, and wives the world over is very bad for you. But you have been following this routine for so long you do not dare stop now and you cringe when you imagine how bad your hangovers would be without the aspirin.

You step into the shower stall with the bottle at your side. You are cautious to keep a hand dry as you tip it back and pour the aspirin into the cup of your palm, and you have counted out four when you spy a large, foreign pill peeking from the bottle's lip and your eyes widen and you exit the stall to pour the bottle's contents onto the countertop. You find four of these white pills mixed in with the aspirin and your heart is breaking with happiness as you eat them. You cannot recall how you came to possess them but you commend yourself for not taking the pills the night before, and you allow yourself to think of your drunken, blacked-out other half not as a man to fear but as one upon whom you would call if you were ever in trouble. This is a fantastic lie but because you are telling it only to yourself you do not feel bad about it.

You return to the stall and your skin is prickly from fatigue and pain and there is a hissing in your ears. Time passes and the pills are taking hold like a glowing white planet coming into view, a reverse eclipse, and you watch with your eyes closed, your body propped in the corner of the stall like a mannequin. There is a knock on the bathroom door but you ignore it. The white planet is half exposed; it grips your heart in its light and seems to be pulling you forward, and now you feel that you are falling. You are awake but dreaming. "The earth is not beautiful but the universe is," you say. Your words reverberate off the green and greener tiles of the shower stall and there are footsteps in the hall and you pretend they are the footsteps of liberating soldiers and you call out to your wife, "Let me take you to the movies," but she does not answer. "I want to go to the movies today," you say, and think again of the rippling, rising curtain in the cold dark room of the theater, and of your wife's soft hand in yours and of her face, not angry and tight as it has been so often lately, but soft and pretty, as when you were courting, and she loved you, when she said she would help you, with freckles on her chin that you could touch with your fingertips anytime you wanted. But what words might you use that would restore your wife's faith in you, when you have used up so many words already, and when the words have all proven false? There are always other words, you tell yourself, there will always be some combination of words that will return your wife's love to you, and you hold your hand to your mouth to hide your smile. There are so many things to be happy about you do not suppose you will ever be sad again.

DISCUSS MERLIN. He is seventy years old, with close-cropped white hair, a long white beard, and desperate, deep-set gray eyes. He chain-smokes brown More cigarettes; they tremble in his spotted, hairy hands or hang from the corner of his lipless mouth and he speaks from behind a screen of smoke, his fingers interlocking like puzzle pieces, a visual aid to some astrological peculiarity or possibly a dirty joke. His teeth are jagged, yellow, and rodent-like, and when he laughs his neck is all veins and tendons and you force yourself to look for no reason other than it is a difficult thing to do.

His vocation is mired in the pall of alcoholic fiction but he claims to be involved alternately in moviemaking, real estate, stock speculation, and something called life coaching, which as far as you can tell is an ugly cousin to psychology requiring considerably less schooling. He speaks of his freelance work as a medium and of his relationship to the other side, hence his nickname, which he is aware of and apparently not offended by. Despite his many professions he is usually broke and twice has asked you for small loans to tide him over until the banks open. "No," you said flatly, and he bared his teeth and retreated like a crab into the shadows of the cold, smoke-filled room.

He is a man in crisis. He favors futuristic, multibuckling sandals and brightly colored nylon jumpsuits, but is known to wear for business purposes a voluminous double-breasted sharkskin suit and tasseled wingtips. These meetings invariably go poorly and Merlin complains of his clients and investors, christening them chickenhearts and babyhearts and yellowbacks. On such nights as these he grinds his fangs and slaps at the bar, cursing the cruel machine called Hollywood with mounting venom until complaints are made and Simon is forced to intervene, clamping Merlin's arm to hush him. Merlin drops his eyes in shame. He is envious of Simon's good looks and accent and he spreads a rumor that Simon was not born in cosmopolitan Johannesburg but the squalor of a desert scrubland, surrounded by "yipping pygmies and hippo shit." Merlin was born in Cincinnati but affects an English accent when drinking.

One night you and Simon are alone in the bar when Merlin, leather fanny pack slung over his shoulder, walks in to greet you. He comments on the empty room: "Ghost Ship," he says. He is suppressing a smile and looks as though he has just found a wallet in the gutter but is hoping to conceal this for fear that someone will claim it. He asks for a drink and you pour him a quadruple vodka and tonic with lime, on the house. This is your new tactic for dealing with hangers-on such as these: You get them helplessly drunk and refuse all money, even tips, and in the morning when they are stuffing chunky bits of vomit down the shower drain with their toes, you hope that they think of you, and that the next time they visit the bar they will ask someone else to serve them. Simon knows what you are doing and he smiles his handsome smile, lowering his head to hide it.

Merlin sucks on a lime wedge and drops the rind into his glass and his shoulders shudder as he drinks and he raises his head to study his reflection in the mirror behind the bar. He lights a cigarette and the smoke slips upward in a slick blue ribbon. Simon asks him what's the latest and Merlin's eyes cloud over; there is lime pulp in his beard and before he speaks he shows you his teeth. "I've just come from a meeting," he says. Simon, nudging you, asks him if his ship's come in, and Merlin says it wasn't that sort of a meeting. An AA meeting, then, Simon says. Merlin shakes his head. "A psychic meeting," you say, and Merlin nods deliberately. He takes another drink and raises his eyes to meet Simon's.

"A round-table vision," he says. "The strongest any of us have ever experienced. You will be murdered in your home on the fifteenth of September. You will be shot twice, once in the brain and once in the heart. The heart shot will kill you but it will take some time to die. The shooter's a nigger, little and mean. He'll never be caught and he'll laugh as he drives away in your car."

Simon is clutching a dishrag. "Mean little . . . what?" he says. His mouth is open, his jaw crooked and stiff. He is wringing the dishrag in his hands.

"You'll die on the burgundy rug in your front room. The light of the morning will be glowing in the windows. The blood pool will expand toward the walls and door. The door is blue. The curtains are beige and a red telephone is ringing. Your voice is on the answering machine greeting and your body is twitching. The caller doesn't leave a message. Your body goes limp, and you die." He takes another drink and gasps. "This is what will happen to you on the fifteenth of September."

Merlin finishes his drink and leaves without tipping. Simon has gone uniformly white and for once has nothing to say. You bring him a large shot of tequila and tell him Merlin is a fool, but he shakes his head and says the description of his apartment was exact. He drinks the tequila and points for another, and then another, and he continues drinking and soon is drunk and by midnight you are helping him into the back seat of a taxi. He is gurgling and cursing Merlin and the driver hands him a plastic bag should he have to vomit. You give the driver the address and watch Simon's head slide from view as the taxi rounds the corner at Santa Monica.

Back in the bar you consult the calendar that hangs above the register and see that Simon has four months and seventeen days left before he will be killed. You mark the date with skull and crossbones and turn to resume your work but the bar is still empty and there is no work to be done, and you stand with your arms crossed and wait for something to happen.

Discuss sam, the bar's principal cocaine dealer, a black man in his mid-forties who grew up with the owner in a nearby suburb. He had hoped to find work at the bar but when it became clear his old friend would not give him any legal position he cornered the stimulant market and now does a brisk business out of a stall in the back bar men's bathroom, this in spite of the fact that he keeps his stash in his gas tank and that his product smells of regular unleaded. He has three small children, sons, who sometimes accompany him to the bar as he works; they circle him and drag their hands down the front of his pant legs, demanding money, colas, chocolate Kisses, their mothers, and beds to sleep in. Sam does not like bringing his sons to the bar but says that at times it is unavoidable. You always take the boys into the manager's office, where there is a television set and a jar of candies, and ask them to stay put because if the fire department or any city employee found them on the premises on a Saturday night the bar would be closed and you would be out of a job and the state would take the children away to institutions and Sam to jail. The other employees complain about him but the owner and the owner's wife tolerate him, not out of any sentiment but because he gives them free drugs whenever it occurs to them to ask. You like Sam and always give him top-shelf vodkas when the others give him the well. His eyes are forever bloodshot and he is terminally exhausted and you imagine his head is stuffed with wood shavings and that he cannot hear a thing you say.

You are alone in the bar in the early evening. Having seen a scary horror movie the night before you sense the ghost lurking around every corner, her cold body hoping to cover yours and chill your blood to slushy ice. You stand near the jukebox (whose lights frighten the ghost) and are punching in songs when you hear the front door open and close and you turn and see the room is empty, which is not uncommon as people often come by to poke their heads in and check for a crowd, but still it frightens you when you think that the ghost might be blocking your escape route. You push this from your mind and are again focusing on the jukebox when the door opens and closes once more, and you turn to find the room still bare, and your heartbeat accelerates and you stare hard at the lights of the jukebox, your eyes crossing, your fingers pressing in songs at random, and you think you sense a slowly approaching body shape at your side and you turn and see the shape is real and you shriek in sincere terror and the shape jumps back and curses and it is not the ghost but Sam. You are so happy you hug him and lift him from the ground and he asks if you are crazy because you looked right at him when he walked in, but he is wearing dark clothes and his skin is dark and the bar is dark and you both laugh at what has happened. "Next time I want you to give a great big smile when you come in," you tell him, and he smiles and his teeth glow like a slivered moon tipped over on its spine.

RAYMOND SITS AT the far right-hand corner of the bar and waves for you to bring him more napkins. He will use an entire stack before night's end, and not for cleaning up. His pens are in a line and he pulls from his pocket a small, jellyfish-colored ruler and he begins to draw, and to drink—whiskey in the winter, tequila in the summertime. If anyone should reach for a napkin from his personal pile he removes their hand and directs them elsewhere; this offends the bar patrons and they ask to view the drawings but Raymond will never allow it. He obscures the napkins with his forearms and hands and squirrels them in a bulging pants pocket, careful not to leave any behind. His hair is brown-gray, his bushy mustache dark brown and silky. He always wears the same T-shirt, which reads ART SAVES LIVES. His glasses sit on the end of a long, sharp nose; his eyes peer over top of the lenses, which gives the impression he is confiding something when he speaks with you. He looks to have been handsome in his youth and in fact is still handsome. His thick hair is swept to the side, by turns boyish and Hitleresque, and he smiles easily and will speak with anyone but gives his attention chiefly to the employees of the bar, to whom he addresses many questions, some of them coherent and motivated by a genuine and good-natured curiosity, others seemingly not. Around the time you first meet him, for example, he asks if you have ever been buried alive. You tell him you never have and he nods and says that everyone should be buried alive at least once in his life, and you make no comment but steal away to busy yourself with an invented task. The query becomes legendary among the bar staff and forever after, whenever a customer asks a foolish question, you ask this person in return if he or she has ever been buried alive.

You ask Raymond what he does for a living and he says, "I breathe and walk and when I'm told to sit I sit and when I'm told to leave I leave and return home to luxuriate and think of how much I despise them." He implies there is a correlation between his daily work and the drawings, which leads people to believe he is some type of an architect, but you suspect there is no place for him with even the most incompetent firm.

He is full of mystery and a looming evil but the strangest thing about Raymond is his choice of shoes. The first time you see them you burst out laughing and leave the room for fear you will offend him. Later you tell Raymond how much you like the shoes and ask if he would mind your sketching them (you are an amateur artist) and he makes a grand gesture of your request, loaning them to you on the spot and walking off into the night barefoot. You take them home and make several ink drawings and later present one to Raymond, along with the tiny, elfin shoes, and he is pleased with the rendering and your interest in his footwear.

COCAINE IS EVERYWHERE and most every employee at the bar will take cocaine while he works. As many times as it has been offered to you and as drunk as you have been you have never, in your many years here, taken cocaine. As a boy in junior high school and then in high school you took every drug under the sun and came to understand, after countless irretrievable days and nights, that stimulants were for the brainless rich, those hoping to jump-start inspiration into their complacent existences. You listened then to the late-night stimulant talk and you listen to it now after hours, the only difference being that those presently fighting for the spotlight are older and even less interested in being alive.

One night, for reasons made invisible by whiskey, you take cocaine. You snort only a small amount but fall victim to the drug and soon it is four-thirty in the morning and you are gasping like a fish out of water, gnashing your teeth and waiting for your turn to speak. There are ten in a circle and everyone wants to speak and no one cares what the person presently speaking is talking about. Someone starts crying about having been molested as a child; someone starts crying about a dead mother; someone wants to go to Las Vegas. You slip out the side door and into your car. It is five-thirty in the morning and the sky is the color of a three-day-old bruise. It is beautiful.

Your wife hears you walking up the steps. She has been waiting for you and is angry and her eyes are fierce as you enter the bedroom and so without a word you turn and walk back down the steps with your bicycle over your shoulder. Your wife is calling your name but you do not answer. You are racing down the steep hill toward Sunset and the rush of cool morning air plucks your cap from your head and drags teardrops across your face and you cannot stop laughing and you wonder why you have not done this before. Cars swerve around you and honk their horns as you veer into traffic; your balance is gone and you hop a curb and soar over the handlebars onto the sidewalk. Looking up at the sky you decide you will ride your bicycle to and from work every night. In a month's time you will be in excellent physical shape and your eyes will glow golden with all they have seen.

You remount the bike and pedal east on Sunset toward downtown. There is a shrieking in your eardrums and you locate a rising lump on your forehead but your fingertips come away free of blood and you carry on. Broadway is in transformation as the shop owners roll up their metal shutters to begin another day of commerce while the addicts, winos, and prostitutes head for their hotels for a few hours' rest. You follow these night crawlers and call out to them in greeting but they do not call back. They are tired and uninterested in all you have seen or think you have seen. They have seen more and their eyes are not glowing golden but gray and lifeless.

Now you too are tired as you pedal back up Sunset. It is warmer and you are dripping with sweat that smells of whiskey and cocaine. Your vision is half black from the blow to your forehead and your body is ringing with pain and you remember your angry, waiting wife and the long hill that you will now have to climb and you wonder why you ever went out for this ride on your bicycle. You will never ride this bicycle again, you decide, and once more you hop a curb and spill over the handlebars. You flag down a man delivering papers in a pickup truck and offer him twenty dollars to take you home and he accepts the money and loads your bicycle in the truck bed atop the newspapers. He does not speak English but whistles at your lump. "No bueno," you say. "Muy borracho." The man nods, and smiles. "Muy borracho," he says. "No bueno." He makes a show of holding his nose at your smell.

Each time you kneel to open the floor safe you think of a rigged heist whereby a friend would rob you and wallop your eyeball to wound you. You would telephone the police and point to the empty safe and your ugly eye and perhaps you would earn a reward for boldness in the face of virulent danger. You imagine a rendezvous afterward, a fine dining experience, a pyramid of money stacks through which you and your friend would spy each other, saying, "Oh boy, oh boy." There would be steak blood and red wine spilled on the restaurant linens and there would be laughter into the night and people would think you were a rich man, and a handsome man—a good enough plan, all in all, except you do not have any friends who would lovingly wallop your eyeball for two thousand dollars. Or rather, those who would could not be trusted to return with the money. But it is a magnetic thing to think about, the emptying of the floor safe, and the image of the creeping blood and wine will always bring a hopeful smile to your face.

Discuss the child actor, now grown, who frequents the bar. He is red and bloated but beneath the bleached hair and tattoos you see traces of the baby face that brought him stardom in his youth. You have trouble looking at him even peripherally and you will never look him directly in the eye for fear that you may come to know him, or that you will see for a moment his inmost being, which you are certain is a staggering, desolate, evil work of nature. His money is almost gone and his former agency no longer sends birthday or Christmas greetings and he buckles down for a suicide bender and asks that the employees of the bar assist him in this. No one knows what to say; no one says anything.

He is often recognized and will always make a fuss about it, as though his prior fame is the last thing in the world he wishes to discuss, when in fact it is the only topic he can speak of with any sort of insight or clarity. He calls you by name and makes sport of his decline, as if it is all in fun that he is drinking himself into a hospital or else to death, and you, hating him, are inspired to help him along: You give him an unlimited supply of well rum and confide that you will never charge him so long as he drinks the rum straight and without any water or cola backs and he agrees to this and can often be found on the floor of the men's room with dried vomit on his oversized flame-patterned button-up shirt. The doormen drag him onto the sidewalk after last call and you step over his sleeping body on the way to your car.

Weeks go by and he shows no sign of slowing down. One night he actually weeps at the bar and you hear him repeating lines from films he starred in and you still cannot look at him and now the sound of his voice is also poisonous. He screams himself hoarse and slaps the bar for another rum; you have just slashed your finger on a broken pint glass and the dripping blood gives you an idea to help him along further. As you pour his drink you point your wounded finger downward and blood trickles in as a mixer. You do this because you hope to give the child actor hepatitis C, a liver disease from which you suffer and will eventually die from. It looks as though you have added a dash of bitters to the rum and this is just what you tell the child actor when he grimaces at his drink's coloring. He tosses back the cocktail and moves to the bathroom to lie on the floor and gurgle, and Curtis drags him past after hours and you watch the child actor's hanging gut and visualize the hepatitis moving toward his liver and covering the inflamed organ like a velvet cloak. His will be a strong disease and he will not know he has it until it is too late, and then he will die, and never bother you for glasses of rum ever again.

Discuss Junior, the black crack addict whose whole world is the sidewalk in front of the bar. He claims to have been a promising college football player with an eye on the NFL. This is probably not true but you must admit he looks the part: He is six and a half feet tall and weighs 350 pounds; that he continues to pack on weight despite his never-ending drug spree is a testament to his miraculous physical inner workings. True or not, you find this story of squandered athletic talent endearing and so decide to believe him or pretend to believe him. Because of this, and because you give him money to wash your car windows when you are drunk, and because you are so skinny and so white, Junior falls platonically in love with you. He picks you up and shakes you and you peer into his open mouth like a boy looking through a hole in a circus tent.

He stammers when he is high and you smile as he struggles to tell his story. He speaks of his therapist and asks for money to visit her and you are quick to support him in this but you wonder does he mean to see her in the morning? Or is she on call twenty-four hours a day? You ask if he is making any progress with the woman and he says she is a great help and that he will continue to see her as she is superbly talented, and after all he is a special case and cannot go to any random therapist. You ask how his case is special and Junior shows you his pendulous, ungainly purple organ. It is one foot long, flaccid. "It's n-not every lady in this world c-c-can sit on that," he tells you.

There are other street elements competing for the crumbs

from the bar patrons and Junior struggles to maintain his crowd. You sometimes visit with these others and find them to be base creatures devoid of charm or hustle. One young addict in particular is utterly stupid and criminal, with nothing behind his eyes but malice and gluttony. He requests cigarettes and money and alcohol in a mumbling monotone and receives them without giving thanks and there is probably something wrong with his brain but you hate him for his uninspired dealings, unlike Junior, who smiles honestly and is happy in his work and with his lot in life and who will wash your car so that it shines brand new.

The young addict corners you and tells you that Junior is a snitch who will be killed and that you should stay away from him because any associates may also be killed. The young addict is just out of jail and says that the car will soon arrive to gun Junior down, who at that moment walks past and the young addict says to him, "Tonight's the night, I hope you're ready to go." You do not believe anyone is coming for Junior and tell him as much, but he is afraid and you return to the bar after he takes you aside and admits he did in fact snitch and that six or more people had gone briefly to jail as a result. There is nothing worse in the world than a snitch and now you are confused in your feelings toward Junior. At midnight a car backfires and you crane your neck to look but you do not hear any screaming on the sidewalk and you bow your head to return to work.

The death car never arrives but at the end of the night you find the young addict and another, older addict blocking Junior's path in the parking lot. They insult him and spit on him and you learn that for all his size he is a coward. His head is down and the spit rains on him and when you ask if he needs a ride the young addict turns and swears to kill you if you do not go away. When you do not leave he moves toward you, and

Junior comes to life, swinging his heavy arm and knocking a Budweiser tall boy out of the young addict's hand, and the beer can hurtles into the night sky and the four of you watch it soar over a billboard and onto the roof of the bar.

The young addict's hand is hurt and he is in a rage and he points to your car and identifies it as yours and says that tomorrow night he will set it on fire. You have every reason to believe him for his eyes are insane with hatred and narcotics, and he turns to Junior and says he will slit his throat as he sleeps, and he names the place where Junior keeps his mattress. Then he brandishes a knife and moves toward Junior in a crouching spider walk and the older addict, following the knife with his custard-colored eyes, says, "Stick him, stick him, stick him," and you shepherd Junior into your car and race off with the two addicts howling at your heels.

Junior cups his head. He is angry with you for your tentative role in his impending murder but you say nothing because you know there is no solution except for him to walk off into the night and hope the young addict is not brave enough to kill another man. You pull the car over in an alley south of Hollywood Boulevard and Junior gathers his rags and Windex bottles and pulls from his bucket a halved machete blade with a duct tape handle. He secrets this beneath his shirt and says goodbye, and you wave and watch him go. There is nothing you can do for him now.

YOU ARE OFTEN DRINKING or drunk but lately are dependent more on beer than whiskey. Your motive is to give aid to your liver, flush the redness from your face and neck, and appease your wife. For a time the campaign is a success: You feel healthier and an unknown energy illuminates your

eyes and limbs and your sleep and appetite are restored, but
the beer is fattening and you gain ten pounds; the weight
sits like a cat on your stomach and your slim profile is blem-
ished. When some happy-hour funnyman asks how far along
you are your vanity is wounded and so it is with great relief
and enthusiasm that you return to whiskey, but in your hia-
tus you have lost your tolerance and the whiskey poisons you
and after a week everything tastes like milk. The whiskey itself tastes like milk, cola tastes like milk, anything you eat or
drink leaves a taste of milk in your mouth. This has happened
before and you are not alarmed, it is merely a sign that you
have passed into the arena where your body has divorced itself from your mind. The mind is the master, the place where
appetites are formed and born; the body is the servant. The
mind has proven to be an unfit leader and the body is taking
measures to protect itself from the mind's desires. For reasons you don't understand or care to understand this has af-
fected your sense of taste.

While the forces of body and mind battle it out, you comfort yourself with the thought that after all you like the taste
of milk and always have, ever since you were a greasy little
baby.

Discuss the teachers, Terese and Terri, who
have been regulars for thirteen years, since the bar first
opened under the present ownership. They are both over six
feet tall and have matching tattoos of worm-ridden apples on
their lower backs that they hide from their students and coworkers but display proudly in the bar. They find you sweet
but unattractive and so you become one of the girls and they
let you in on all their secrets. Between the two of them they

have slept with most every doorman who has ever worked at the bar and they tell you which ones have mirrors on their ceilings and which insist on videotaping their sexual encounters. These tapes are traded back and forth and the doormen throw parties where they watch the tapes together and afterward eat barbeque and critique one another's performances. Some take steroids and are suffering the drugs' side effects: Their genitals have shriveled away to nothing and they have grown small breasts, which The Teachers call bitch tits. One doorman has become particularly buxom and is said to wear a sports bra that he made at home from Ace bandages.

The Teachers drink salted margaritas one after the other until they are cross-eyed and you cannot imagine them instructing and caring for young children in the preschool where they work but this is just what they do. They pride themselves on never drinking on the job (you think this is a lie) and they say that if you too would refrain you might see yourself promoted and they remind you how old you are and how long you have been working at the bar and they shake their heads out of pity for your wife. They say you wouldn't be half bad-looking if only you would work out. If you could add, say, thirty pounds of muscle to your upper body, the chest in particular, you would be something of a catch. You thank The Teachers for their stories and advice and you promise to bring your to-be-born child to their preschool and they say they would be happy to have him/her but they hope you will hold off procreating until you have been promoted, and until you have given some thought to what they have said about your weight. "A father should have some muscle behind him," Terese says.

"You don't look like a father to me," Terri tells you.

They hold up their hands for two more margaritas.

DISCUSS MONTY AND MADGE, a pair of drifter types made strange and unknowable by a lifetime of vodka and cold shoulders. Monty is thirty years old and unwashed, his glasses Scotch-taped, his burgundy corduroy dress coat dirty at its cuffs; he gives off the unmistakable psychic odor of a man who has lived in institutions and by-the-hour motels. He is eager to talk but his conversations are limited to the subjects of alcohol and movies, his obsessions and apparent motives for carrying on. He drinks double vodka tonics from the well and becomes animated when describing a stunt or special effect from the latest Hollywood blockbuster. When he insists you see these movies you tell him you do not like the genre and he asks what other kinds there are and you say there are the slow ones and foreign ones and your personal favorites, the sad ones, and he blinks and says that there are two types of people: Those who want to cry, and those who are crying already and want to stop.

Madge has never said a word to you or (as far as you know) to Monty and you believe she is presently insane. A light-skinned mulatto, she resides beneath a ratty gray beehive hairdo and behind a pair of neon-green gas-station sunglasses. Her face is heavily rouged, her lipstick smeared over tiny gray teeth; she is perhaps twenty years older than Monty and the exact nature of their relationship remains clouded. He orders her drinks (well bloody marys) and always pays and she accepts the drink in her hand but has not once thanked him and in fact has never looked in his direction. She drinks slowly but steadily and Monty anticipates each drink's completion so that she is never left wanting or thirsty. She chain-smokes unfiltered Lucky Strikes and her fingers are stained an unladylike yellow-brown.

When happy hour is over and prices double it is time to go and Monty taps Madge's shoulder and without moving her neck she stands and turns and walks out the door. Madge embarrasses Monty and he apologizes each time they visit. "She's just a shy girl is all," he explains. "Time's been hard on her." Then he settles the bill, and here is the most curious thing about Monty: He is a good tipper. If he saved the tips from a single happy hour he could buy himself a nice secondhand coat. A week's worth would get him a new pair of eyeglasses. But he enjoys the pageantry of public drinking and appreciates your remembering his name and interests, and when he reaches for his wallet you want to refuse his money but can see how much the gesture means to him and so you only thank him and stuff the cash in the tip jar.

You are alone in the bar with Monty and Madge when a man walks in and sits on the stool nearest the television. He is of medium height, brown-haired, muscular and tanned, the archetypal Southern Californian in shorts and a frayed T-shirt advertising a marlin-fishing tournament in Baja. There is a baseball game on and you peg him for a sports fan when you see how intently he watches the screen, but then he is interested in the commercials too, and when you walk over to take his order he jumps at the sound of your voice. He turns his washed-out blue eyes to you and you see he is simple or crazy or drunk or on drugs. He looks to Monty and Madge (Monty waves, Madge makes a wet, farting noise with her mouth) and back at you. The game has resumed and he points to the screen.

"How much do these baseball players make?" he asks.

It seems an innocent-enough question on its surface but the fact that he is unaware each player is paid a different salary worries you as it reveals the man's separation from reality. Anyway you do not believe he is interested in the actual answer and so you say, "Plenty more than you or me," and he grins crookedly. He flattens several crumpled bills on the bar and asks what he can get for six dollars and you pour him a vodka tonic that he drains in a gulp. He does not tip but pulls more bills from his pocket and likewise flattens these and asks what he can get for ten dollars. You make him a double vodka tonic and again he does not tip. He drains the glass and asks what he can get for twenty dollars and you are becoming frustrated and tell him for that much he could buy the whole bar a round, but the man is confused and then offended by your joke, and his eyes flash and he stares at your chest and says, "Why would I buy you all drinks when I don't even know you? When I don't even know your names? Why in the fuck would I give you a goddamn thing?" His fists are clenched and he has stood and kicked aside his stool and it looks as if he wants to jump over the bar when Monty calls out from across the room: "Just give him a drink on my tab. Give him whatever he wants."

At these words the man gradually uncoils. He loosens his fists and rights his stool and moves to sit beside Monty. He orders another double vodka tonic, smiling now as though nothing has happened, and he thanks you when you bring the drink over. His name, he says, is Joe, and he shakes Monty's hand and extends a hand to Madge, who makes a kissing sound but otherwise does not acknowledge him. (Joe does not appear to think this strange.) The three of them become fast friends and throughout the night you hear Joe asking Monty questions:

"How do you make a baby sleep if it doesn't want to sleep?"

"How much do electric razors cost?"

"What *is* death rock?"

"How does rice grow? Do you know what I mean? How does it *grow*?"

Monty answers as well as he can, all the while buying drinks for the group. Joe moves in closer and when Monty calls him a curious boy, Joe says that he is very curious indeed, and he rests a hand on Monty's, and five minutes later they stand and leave the bar together. Things are strange and just got stranger and Madge remains behind, her arm working to drain her glass and then the partially full glasses of Monty and Joe, and you say to her, "Looks like it's just you and me, Madgey." Her drinks are empty and you bring her another on the house. Sucking on a Lucky Strike, she fills her cheeks with smoke and exhales in your face. She raises the drink to her lips.

MONTY NOW PAYS for Joe's movies and drinks in addition to Madge's and his own, and his tips disappear, and he does not speak to you anymore about his favorite special effects and will no longer look you in the eye. He is in love with Joe and grasps his hand beneath the bar and becomes jealous if Joe should look at or speak with any women. Joe does not love Monty and you suspect he is not much interested in men but only playing a part until something more agreeable comes along. Sometimes he leaves with these bar women and Monty's heart breaks; he swears his revenge on the whores of the world and drinks well past happy hour, gleefully spending the money that would be Joe's, saying to Madge that it's just the two of them now, like before, but the next day or the day after Joe will be back, grinning and crazy in his eyes, with Monty at his side, swooning at Joe's dimples and Roman profile. Madge for her part is unaffected by the drama, though she now sits one stool away from her drinking partners and seems for unknown reasons to have warmed to you and once even smiled in your direction when you were doing a funny dance for Simon.

Toward the end of each month when his welfare money and medications have run out Joe begins acting erratically and will usually by the twenty-ninth or thirtieth have thrown a fit and been ejected from the bar. These episodes sometimes happen quickly, in the time it takes to smash a pint glass on the floor, and you will look up to find Joe screaming at the television or the ceiling or into a void, a dark space in the room. Other times his mood will deteriorate in slow stages throughout the night: He will enter the bar with his frenzied eyes and sit with his drink, enthusiastic about his good fortune and friends, when some imperceptible injustice captures his attention and poisons the very soil of his earth, and his conversation drops off and he will begin brooding, then mumbling, then cursing and shouting, and then he will be tossed onto the sidewalk where he will wail and punch holes in the sky. You come to recognize Joe's warning signs and give him room to offend or be offended by someone other than yourself—a lone customer or one of the other bar employees or, as is usually the case, Monty, who afterward is left behind to apologize and pick up glass shards and pay for any damages. Although it is part of your job description to suppress any violence until security arrives, you do not intervene in Joe's tantrums because you have become truly afraid of his eyes and you believe it is only a matter of time before he kills someone, and you do not want to die at the bar, at the hands of a man in flip-flops and a Señor Frog's poncho.

Monty can no longer support both the drinking and cinema habits of this unfortunate crew, and they forgo the movies to spend afternoons and early evenings at the bar. The omission of entertainment in their lives takes its toll on their self-esteem, and Monty and Joe no longer speak to each other except to order drinks or comment on certain television happenings, and so begins their comprehensive degeneration: Monty's every move and gesture is motivated by money and love worries. His hygiene, already dubious, falls further into decline so that people grimace at his approach and gather their things as he sits down beside them. Unaware, Monty jabs his thumbs into his temples, suggesting unchecked and tacit pain. When Joe sits beside him, Monty wants to moan—the unobtainable prize, Joe is now openly on the lookout for another meal ticket. He has become commonly cruel, and will order top-shelf vodkas for the sport of watching Monty's wretched, shivering reaction. Monty holds his wallet like a sick bird and you see in his eyes he will be driven crazy by hopeless love if he cannot slow the process down somehow.

As interesting as all this is, you find yourself focusing more and more on Madge, studying her in secret, and you begin to get an idea about her that you cannot shake, an idea you decide you must get to the bottom of, but in order to do this you will have to speak with her, and you begin asking her questions about her childhood and hometown and mother and father, though she will not so much as nod at you. You tell her that if she will only say her full Christian name aloud you will give her drinks on the house for the entire night up until closing time, and her head jerks and her mouth creaks open but she does not make a noise. Then you offer her drinks on the house until she is dead if she will only say the word *hello*, and you see that she is heated to the marrow of her bones by the thought of it, and yet she still says nothing but stands stiffly and walks out the door and does not return again that night. (Monty and Joe heard this last offer and are both shouting "Hello! Hello! Hello!" at you.)

The idea you have about Madge is that she is a man, and this is confirmed the next night when she walks into the bar, alone and sober, and tells you in a deep voice that Monty and Joe have hatched a plan to hit you with a club and rob you, and that they will arrive in half an hour to do just this. She says that Joe is all-the-way crazy and speaks about killing constantly and once went after her with a Swiss Army knife. Monty is half crazy and will do whatever Joe says so long as they stay together. She says they have been up for three days on bad amphetamines and that you must lock the door at once and wait for them to move on, but the idea of Joe knocking hard on the door with you alone in the darkened bar is too much to bear and you are walking toward the phone to call the police but Madge becomes alarmed and begs you not to, saying that she loves Monty, that she is all alone, and that Joe will soon be dead or in jail and then her and Monty's life will return to its former harmonious state. She is crying and you tell her you are sorry but will simply have to call the police, and she coughs through her tears and says that she knows another way, and she borrows a pen and writes this out on a napkin:

Dear Montgomery,
   The bartender knows cuz I told him. I'm sorry but Joe's a low-down Dog and I love you and you will Die if you go back to Prison. I am leaving this town but will write c/o your Mom once I get somewhere.
Goodbye now,
Tim

Madge dries her face and asks for a piece of tape to stick the note on the front door, only there is no tape and she says she will use a piece of chewing gum. You walk her out and you lock the door behind her and wait. Three cigarettes later you hear this: Footsteps approaching, crinkling paper, a murmur of voices, and the sound of footsteps hurriedly retreating. You will not see Monty, Madge, or Joe at the bar again.

It is september 15, the day Simon is to be murdered in his front room, and a group of regulars and bar employees gather in his apartment to watch over him throughout the night. The Teachers arrive bearing medical supplies, margarita mix, and a blender. Next comes Curtis. He is wearing his usual policeman getup along with a pair of silver and gold spurs attached with string to his worn brown loafers. "They blow the look but still sound cool," he says. He is saving up for a pair of motorcycle-cop boots. Behind him is the child actor. He looks a little yellow and you rush over to ask about his health. Is he experiencing any lapses in energy? Any pains in his right side beneath the rib cage? Does he find that surface wounds are taking an abnormally long time to heal? He says he is feeling fine. He is on call for a Where Are They Now game show that pays fifteen thousand dollars per episode. He will never forget what you've done for him, he says, and when the checks start rolling in you can be sure he'll be spending his money at the bar. You sigh, and return to the corner with your whiskey. You notice a familiarity between the child actor and Curtis and it dawns on you that they spend time together outside of the bar. You can see them sipping morning beers in San Fernando Valley strip clubs and you dig your palm heels into your eye sockets and make a long wheezing sound. Curtis finds a NASCAR race on television and turns this up so loud it sounds as if the cars are in the room with you.

Merlin shows up with a case of warm Pabst and is grudgingly admitted—there is an unspoken belief that he has an unnatural hand in Simon's forthcoming demise. Simon has already drunk a bottle and a half of wine and his eyes are glazed and he is confused by Merlin's arrival. "What are you doing here?" he asks. Merlin shrugs. Simon will drink himself into oblivion tonight. "What are you doing here, mate?" he asks you. "I'm here to kill your killer," you say, and he smiles, and thanks you. He is drinking from the bottle now.

The doormen arrive and display their weapons: Flick knives, handguns, brass knuckles, Mace, a sawed-off shotgun, and a canister of tear gas. The notion that someone may soon be killed is intoxicating to the group and they gather around a large pile of cocaine like wiggling piglets on a tit. All are indulging save for Merlin and Simon and yourself. You are watching Merlin who is watching Simon who is watching the door. Merlin is smiling with smug satisfaction; Simon looks as though he will cry or shout out in pain and for the first time since you have met him you can read his true age, the untold years lingering about his eyes and mouth. You are not sure if it is the lighting in the apartment or his present concerns but he does look like a man about to die. "What are you doing here?" he asks again. "You're going to be murdered tonight," you tell him. "Oh," he says. He looks at Merlin and then back at the door.

The room is nearly full when two prostitutes arrive. No one will admit to ordering them but you suspect Curtis and the child actor are responsible. They say nothing, lest they are forced to pay. When the women are inside, a doorman fluent in their language steps forward to begin the haggling process. He says he wants to go "around the world," and you, not understanding, envision a kind of pinwheel to which he will be attached and, you suppose, flayed. The prostitutes name a price and the doorman asks what it will cost for everyone other than the suddenly silent Teachers to also make the trip, and after a head count and private conference between the two professionals a price of two thousand dollars is reached. The doorman takes up a collection and hands over one thousand in mangled tens and twenties. He says he will return in half an hour with the other thousand; he orders the prostitutes to strip and dance in the interim and he exits the apartment at a run, whooping shrilly. (This noise is upsetting to Simon. In the back of his mind he knows there is some approaching danger and wonders if this sound is the indication of its onset. He is gripping his chest and panting and this is when you fall platonically in love with him.)

The prostitutes are now naked, and the uglier of the two—they are both very ugly—sits on the armrest of your chair and asks in a husky voice how exactly you are going to fuck her. She is not interested in your answer and is only looking for a simple adjective before moving down the line but her breasts are like rocks in socks and a purple cesarean scar divides her belly and you are laughing uncontrollably. She calls you a slimy faggot and moves on to Curtis, who is beckoning from the couch, waving a phony police badge. She sits on his lap and he takes out his erection—patchily depigmented, you notice, like his hands—but the prostitute will not touch it until the doorman arrives with the rest of the money. The child actor is watching Curtis's erection and barking. He pours beer on it and Curtis howls over the roar of cars on the television. The child actor begins howling. Everyone is howling.

The doorman shows up with the money—he will not say how he got it, though it is understood it was not taken from his own savings—and the prostitutes get on their hands and knees beside each other. They are penetrated from behind while fellating men in front of them and you watch this much in the way one watches gory surgery on television. Everyone is on cocaine and cannot ejaculate and the prostitutes cannot get a word in edgewise and are being worked like plow horses.

There is a hiccup in the party when Curtis begins sodomizing one of the prostitutes without first asking; he is reprimanded and sent to the back of the line to change his condom. He is still wearing his sunglasses and loafers and you tell him how much you like his spurs and he thanks you. He is listlessly masturbating.

In the far corner, away from the others, sit Merlin and Simon and The Teachers. You walk over and Merlin reaches for your whiskey but the thought of his mouth on your bottle displeases you and you snatch it away, handing it to Simon before emptying it yourself, saying to Merlin's glare, "Did you want some? You should have said so." Merlin says nothing but shows you his teeth. The Teachers are upset about the presence of the prostitutes and Terri says that they are nothing but a couple of whores. You think it is humorous to call a prostitute a whore, and you laugh, and Terri tells you to shut up and begins trembling and then crying and you do not know why, and you do not care why. You return to your chair.

One by one you hear the men drop off until only the child actor is left pumping away. His body is red and hairless and he looks like an enormous newborn baby and his prostitute's grunting face is buried in the carpet—her thighs are trembling and it looks as though she will soon collapse. At last he finishes and falls in a heap by the front door, which you notice is slowly, evenly opening. A small black boy is standing in the doorway looking in at the party and Merlin, seeing this, jumps from his chair and screams, "Mean little nigger!" The boy is shocked by what he has just been called and by the state of the room—the child actor groaning and cursing, the prostitute with her flushed backside still in the air, the pile of cocaine and weapons on the coffee table—and his mind rushes to make sense of it all. But he has little time to ponder as the doormen, some partially clothed, some still naked, are gathering weapons to slay him. He is chased down the street and you hear him shrieking as he goes, and Simon staggers after them, shouting that the boy is only his neighbor's son and that he isn't mean at all. "He wouldn't hurt a housefly," he tells you. One of his eyes is closed, the other is bloodshot.

The two prostitutes are standing naked in the kitchen, gargling with mouthwash and wiping themselves with tissues. They are talking about the finer points of common-law marriage, also the difficulties of child rearing. "Once the state gets ahold of your kids, there's nothing to do but say a prayer and make some more," one says, and the other slowly nods. Crossing back to his seat Simon gets his feet tangled in a pair of pants and falls head-first onto the corner of the table, knocking himself out. The curtains are illuminated with the first light of the morning and Simon's blood spreads across the floor and toward the walls. The door is blue. You look for a telephone and find a red one on the floor beside the couch. You jump when it begins ringing. Simon's feet are twitching and Merlin rushes out the door with his few remaining Pabsts under his arm. You pick up the telephone and say hello. The Teachers enter the room and begin screaming.


THE NEW TENANTS discover Curtis in their closet and force him onto the street where he is robbed of his leather jacket, mirrored sunglasses, and holsters—he throws his spurs into the gutter and spits. He spends the next three days and nights blubbering in anonymous alleyways, plotting revenge killings and elaborate suicide parades that he hasn't the intelligence, energy, or courage to execute. Looking in the phone book he finds that his parents, whom he has not seen in many years, are living in the San Fernando Valley, and he calls them collect to plead his case. His mother refuses to fetch him but says she will permit a visit or short stay if he can find his own way, and he throws himself at the mercy of an MTA driver who tells him he can ride for free so long as he stops crying and sits in the rear of the bus. Curtis locates the house and finds his parents sipping Arnold Palmers on a creaking porch swing, a gentle vision that fills his heart with heat and gratitude, only his parents are not happy to see him and are quick to remind him of his many faults and his weird sex escapades. They point to a corner of the garage, a chalk-drawn outline that is to be his living space; they give him a list of chores and tell him that if he should ever fail to complete them he will be immediately and permanently banished from his parents' home and affections. He signs the list and a rental agreement and weeps like Christ on the cross as he mows the dead lawn.

EACH YEAR AT CHRISTMAS you drink whiskey sours for two weeks. The bar smells of pine boughs and glows red and green with Christmas lights and you are reminded of a time several years back when you lived in the North. It was cold and rainy and you were a laborer and this was your drink, whiskey sour with a cherry and a lemon wedge. At night you met with friends at the corner bar and spoke of the little daily things: An accident on the work site, a prank played, things you had stolen from the home of your employer, something unfortunate your sociopathic uncle had done. There was a young woman behind the bar; you liked to watch her reach. She sold you pills over the counter, so when you entered the bar you would shake the rain off your hat and Pendleton coat and say, "Double whiskey sour and two blues, please." You would dry your hands on your pants so as not to dissolve the pills and in twenty minutes would be overcome with a wonderful, fleeting sadness. A string of Christmas lights blinked year round over the bar, which is why you are reminded of your time there each December. You still get calls and invitations to visit the northern town but you don't dare return, as some piece of the memory would certainly be ruined. Everything changes and rarely for the better. But you honor this faraway place with two weeks' worth of whiskey sours at the close of every year, and this will have to do for now.

THERE IS AN UPHEAVAL at the bar motivated by some mysterious money troubles of the owners, who call an emergency daytime meeting and are grim and cryptic as they talk of their finances, and your hands are buzzing at the thought of termination and as the meeting progresses you do not follow along but scramble to think of another occupation you might fall back on, only there is no other occupation except that of laborer or cashier and you cannot return to either as you have been spoiled by barbacking, which leaves your days free and for which you are paid illegally in cash and during which time you can drink all the Jameson you like, and so you decide you will not search out further employment but apply for every existing brand of credit card and then borrow cash advances from each company that agrees to do business with you. You could survive a year if you are careful with your spending, and you think of short trips to Big Sur and San Francisco and cheap hotels and coach train travel. You could even bring a backpack and sleep on the beach like a dirty hippie, or maybe actually *become* a dirty hippie, and you imagine yourself with a beard and a dog and a walking staff and you laugh out loud and the meeting comes to a halt and you apologize and the owners carry on, and now you are listening and this is what you hear them say:

No one is to be terminated (your freewheeling plans are dashed over rocks) but there will be cutbacks, and all employees will have to reel things in until the money troubles recede. This means: The bartenders and barbacks will cease handing out any complimentary drinks, no matter the customer or amount of time or money they have spent at the bar. The employees are aghast at this and begin naming certain customers, saying, You don't mean so-and-so, and We can't be expected to charge such-and-such, and the owners reiterate: Every person pays every dollar for every drink. The decree sinks in and the employees are quiet as they imagine the many horrible conversations they will soon have to have, because to deny the regulars their alcohol would be like turning away hungry bums at a soup kitchen, and you think of their pushed-in faces as you tell them this new rule and again interrupt the meeting with your laughter and you are warned— once again and you're out.

Further rulings: Simon will no longer be manager and his extra pay will hereafter be forfeit. No one says anything to this but wonders why the news of his wage cut was not left to implication. Simon is not in attendance, having been earlier informed of his demotion and spared the public humiliation.

"Is he all right?" you ask.

"He is golfing."

"Who will be the manager now?"

The room comes to attention and the owner and his wife look at each other nervously. They say there is someone they want you all to meet and they call out a name and a golden-tanned young man, dirty blond hair and green-eyed and good-looking to the point of prettiness, enters from the backroom office and stands before the group. This is Lancer; he will be the new manager. He makes the rounds, shaking hands and proffering small compliments (to you he says it is his understanding that you "know how to have some fun"). He is younger than you by a decade and younger than some of the bartenders by two, which means he was still in high school when you began working at the bar and that he was ten years old when the others signed on at the bar's opening. Having no ambition to ascend even to bartender, much less to the position of manager, you are not bothered by this turn of events, but the others in the room are transparently wounded and they stand and shout out and one tips his chair and quits on the spot and the owners raise their arms in a call for peace and for a moment you think there will be violence against them (you will not take part but neither will you play diplomat) and also against Lancer, who has backed himself into the corner and looks uneasy and unnerved (and dramatic and handsome).

There is no violence. The employees drift out the door, ignoring the beckoning voices of the owners and returning to their cars and homes to speak with their wives or girlfriends of the many years sacrificed in the darkness of the bar, all to be passed over for youth, beauty, and inexperience—all for nothing. The owners retire to the office where they will drink away their guilt and you are left alone with Lancer. He is upset about his reception and says he will not take the job but return to his unemployment insurance and his acting and scriptwriting and you are impressed with his manner of communicating this, which is something like a one-way radio and wholly for his own theatrical benefit, and you know there is nothing you can say to this person that will affect him in any way and so you only pat his arm and offer him a drink and he answers this by *looking at his watch*. You walk over to fix yourself a drink and Lancer sees this and says, fine, let's have the one drink and then I'll go and tell the owners to find somebody else, and you bring over two shots of Jameson and he chokes on his and you shiver down the long length of your spine and he asks what the drink was and you tell him the brand and he says no, I mean what type of alcohol, and here you fall platonically in love with Lancer and shout the answer in his face: "Irish whiskey!"

Discuss Brent the unhappy doorman. He is unhappy because: He would rather not be a doorman and because his pigeon-toed bowling-pin-shaped girlfriend leaves him once a month to sleep with his closest friends, whom he dislikes, and who dislike him. He is also unhappy because he suffers from an intestinal disorder whose symptoms are too dire to describe but that he describes often, in precise detail—the malady makes his job of standing in a fixed public location dangerous bordering on torturous. His primary shattering dream is to be a boxer or wrestler or cage fighter—any type of recognized tough, but this will not be realized because Brent is five feet two inches tall and despite his constantly working out and injecting growth hormones he will never attain the desired stature of the truly intimidating violence professional. His secondary shattering dream is to produce cable television shows and during his first two years at the bar this is all he ever speaks of (he is not yet the unhappy doorman but the optimistic, superior doorman). At one point he is close to having a show made into a pilot and he tells you about the many meetings and lunches he attends and he begins using conspicuous Hollywood phrases like *spec* and *soft-scripting* and *postproduction,* and when he speaks of these things he is animated and gleeful and he says that when he receives his first check he will kiss it like a sweetheart, his ticket out of the bar and a lifetime of dirty ID cards, graceless fistfights, smoke-stinking T-shirts, and cymbal-crashing hangovers.

But now his Hollywood banter tapers off and in a few months this talk of *miniplots* and *antiplots* and *greenlights* is a thing of the past and it is understood that his deal has fallen through. He begins to drink on the job and is always motioning for you to bring him secret shots of vodka and he does not care to hear about how busy you are and grows frantic if you leave his glass empty for too long and by last call he is belligerent and unnecessarily forceful in clearing out the bar and as soon as the customers have gone he rushes to the bathroom to suffer under his intestinal condition, the effects of which you can hear, and you hurry over to the jukebox cash in hand to drown out the sound of his sickness.

Lancer does not return to unemployment insurance but takes up his post at the bar, steeled by a pay raise and the belief he will soon move on to bigger and better things. His reception among the customers and employees, Simon in particular, is at first chilly, but he is not concerned; his agent sees great things in his future which he parrots for you and the bartenders, most of whom are actors or ex-actors themselves who have heard similar chatter from their own agents and ex-agents, and they explain to him that these are lies perpetrated by all agents everywhere, and that bolstering a client's ego through deceit is the agent's primary function. Lancer chalks this talk up to sour grapes. "I'm sympathetic," he says. "How would *you* feel after fifteen years of failure?"

"Ask me in five years," you say. But you agree with his

agent—Lancer *is* out of place at the bar, and he probably *will* move on to bigger and better things. His features are too fine, his heart too clean, unblemished by envy and gluttony and self-hatred, to stand in such a room as this for very long. And just as he hopes to leave the bar and surround himself with similarly scenic people, you and the others also want to see him go, that you might forget such a set of teeth ever existed, and that you could continue on without the constant reminder of what was missing from your genetic makeup.

Lancer has been at the bar six months and is now more or less an accepted member of the staff. He is teased but only playfully and his orders, previously ignored, are now followed if not to the letter then at least close to the letter. Even Simon has warmed to him after Lancer got him an audition with his agency. But one person remains critical of him, and that is Brent the unhappy doorman, who at the start of their relationship acted the part of the condescending Hollywood elder, one who had dealt with the big boys and lived to tell the tale, but as his own life falls apart he no longer hides his jealousy and becomes overtly nasty. He hopes to rally the employees against Lancer but this campaign has a reverse effect, the group feeling being that anyone who can arouse such disfavor from a person like Brent must not be all bad. And so it is with something resembling sadness that the bar says goodbye to Lancer during his tenth month of employment—he has sold his movie script and is taking his parents on a Hawaiian vacation before settling into a life of wealth and flashbulbs. The employees are gathered around him at the end of his last night when Brent walks up and asks what the cause of celebration is. When Lancer turns and tells him, Brent winces and sputters that the script will be put on a shelf and forgotten and that he will be back tending bar within a year—shocking behavior, even for someone as miserable as Brent, and the group is struck dumb by so blatant a display of bitterness. Brent too is quiet. He seems startled by his own declaration, and before anyone can gather their wits to chastise him he pretends he had only been joking and that he is actually glad for Lancer and he extends his hand and Lancer takes it up and Brent asks what the script sold for and Lancer names a number in the mid six figures and Brent once again winces and says he does not believe it and Lancer drops a copy of *Variety* on the bar for him to check the amount. Finding that the article corresponds with Lancer's price, Brent staggers backward, breathing heavily, then rushes for the exit, grabbing a barstool on his way out and kicking the door open with his boot. As the door swings closed, you and the others in the group, your necks identically craned, can see him hoist the stool over his head and smash it to bits on the sidewalk.

Discuss the very tall man, whom you see or think you see as you drive up Echo Park Avenue one night on your way home from work. The moon is full and low and shadows fall in such a way that you glimpse from the corner of your eye the silhouette of a man as tall as a single-story building. He is leaning against the wall of a convenience store and you see his wide hat and dark clothing and know he could cross the street to your car in two long strides and you think of him following you home and crawling through your front door on his hands and knees. You begin to dream of him hiding outside your house and your greatest fear is to think of him looking in a window when you are home alone. His hat would slowly come into view through the darkness and trees and bushes and you would lock eyes with him and he would show his teeth and point to the front door.

IGNACIO DOES NOT DRINK, but like the others is in attendance every night. He is a Spanish expatriate in his mid-fifties, a mechanic living in the comfort of his ailing aunt's guesthouse. For reasons that remain obscure he is heavily medicated. He suffers from dizzy spells and sometimes leans against the bar for support and his eyes bulge from their sockets and he once passed a hand over his face and told you, "I am not a handsome man." This was only a piece of another throwaway bar story whose plot you no longer remember, but each time you greet Ignacio you are reminded of this proclamation. It was a magnificent thing to say and you admire him for his self-knowledge.

His coat and shirt are pressed, his shoes shined, his bald head buffed and bright, and his mustache trimmed to fine points—Ignacio is terrifically vain. He has fashioned a pair of pants from heavy leather and adorned them with patches of his own design: Horseshoes, steer heads, shooting stars, and moonbeams. The pants lace up in the back and you wonder whose job it is to help him tie off the garment. Pointing to the leather, you tell him he is bulletproof and he shakes his head. "Asshole-proof," he says. His laughter is like the barking of a dog.

He is a world-class inventor of facts and you enjoy watching him improvise scenarios from a distant, fabricated past. To hear him tell it he has bedded numberless insatiable beauties in Europe, Asia, and North America, and physically humiliated any man who dared show him less than the utmost respect. He claims to have been a bullfighter in his youth and once showed you an old blurry snapshot of himself in full matador garb and cape, standing beside a just-killed bull in the center of a large arena, the ecstatic crowd at his back. You were momentarily impressed with the picture but he would not let you hold it and was suspiciously eager to put it away and later you wondered, was it your imagination or did his cape look more like a baby's blanket? And why were those men in the background rushing toward him? And was he wearing tennis shoes? He will never let you see the photo again, though you ask him every time you see him.

There are certain patrons of the bar whose stories leave you feeling lonely, even bitter, but Ignacio's tales have a luminosity about them and you lean in to catch each word. You know he is a liar but there is something about the stories that seems plausible. He is, or was, open to greatness—there is potential greatness in his eyes—only he was never actually visited by the greatness and so he speaks of what his life would have been like if he had been. He is compulsive about the telling of the stories in that he understands no one believes him and yet he continues to invent and deliver them. Also it seems there is a part of him that listens to his own stories and anticipates their endings, some piece of his being disconnected from its rational core so that he becomes his own rapt audience.

He paints in his spare time, finishing a canvas or two a year, a meager output for even the most relaxed weekend artist, but in his defense the paintings are exceedingly ambitious, if not in their subject matter then in their size, some of them measuring up to ten feet in length and six feet in height. They are pleasant to look at, if a little redundant—circles within circles within circles—but you get the feeling Ignacio is not interested in the finished product so much as the process of seeing a project through to its end. He brings in photos of the completed paintings (he is always posing at their side) and is careful not to let anyone touch them in case they should smudge the images. He moves down the line of regulars, holding the photos at eye level until the viewer sufficiently praises his efforts, and when there is no one else to show he returns the picture envelope to his coat's breast pocket and levels a stubby finger in your direction. Now, despite his doctor's explicit warnings, he will drink one glass of red house wine, and it will take him near an hour to finish and afterward he will not give up the glass but sniff it and lick at its rim.

It is after one of these rare picture-sharing evenings that you ask Ignacio if he has ever worked on a smaller scale and he nods in the affirmative but is slow in elaborating and you see that he is inventing something. It takes some time to work it all out but in a moment he calls you back, and this is the story he tells you:

Early one morning, ten summers past, he was prepping a large canvas in the backyard of his aunt's house. From his work area he could see the happenings on the sidewalk and he noticed a young girl peering through the gates to watch him. She was a beautiful little Hispanic girl, eight or nine years old, and he turned and smiled at her and called for her to come closer, but she was shy and afraid of his deep voice and she ran off. The next morning Ignacio saw she had returned, only this time she passed through the gates and across the property line, and again he greeted her, and again she fled, a routine that continued for a week or more, with the girl getting closer every day until finally she gathered her courage and approached Ignacio to tell him how curious his painting made her, and how much she looked forward to seeing its completion, and she wondered, did he have many other paintings? And did they sell for a million dollars? And why did he paint only shapes and not "things"? And was he a very famous artist? The girl was full of questions, and Ignacio, touched by her innocence, answered them all and asked in turn about her family and life and religion, and her answers were always forthright and charming, and he was glad to be speaking with her, and she with him, and they became friends.

Now she came by every day, pulling up a bucket (it came to be called her bucket) to watch the painting's progress and to talk with him about her days. Ignacio learned of a neighborhood boy whom she loved named Eddie, a rough boy with a cowlick who teased her and called her Ladybones because she was underweight. One day Eddie kissed her cheek, and she shrieked with wild joy and slipped from her bucket as she recounted the episode for Ignacio, but later Eddie kicked her in the stomach and she was heartsick and swore off love for a life devoted to art and the church. She became intent and serious about the painting and her eyes were unblinking and her chatter tapered off and months later when the painting was finished she cried because she didn't want her time with Ignacio to end or for the painting to be moved from its blocks. She wanted the painting for her own, and was inconsolable when she discovered Ignacio had a buyer lined up and that it would be shipped to New York City the very next day.

What the girl did not know was that Ignacio had been spending his nights working on a smaller painting just for her, a special little painting with hearts in the corners and an admiring dedication at the bottom, and when he presented it to her she wiped the tears from her face and placed a hand on the canvas and after a pause began to cry all over again, and she swore before God and Jesus Christ she would someday repay him and she ran off with the canvas under her arm, ashamed of her emotion, and Ignacio laughed as he watched her go and was warm in his body from the good deed he had done.

Now Ignacio bows his head for a sip of soda water and you breathe a great sigh of relief, because for a moment you were afraid this would be a dirty and immoral pedophile love story, and you thank him for the tale and stand to return to your work but he clears his throat and says there is a ways to go yet and to hold your horses because the story soon gets good, and he winks, and you are revisited by your worry. Ignacio strokes his mustache and continues.

"I looked for her every day, but she didn't come by anymore after that. After a while I forgot about her. Years passed, my work continued, when one morning just this last summer I was kneeling in the driveway washing the wheels of my van when I felt a presence at my back, and I could see in the reflection of the hubcaps that there was a woman standing over me, and I turned, and there was a pair of beautiful brown ankles blooming like flowers out of red leather high-heeled shoes. I looked up and saw the calves, and the kneecaps, and the thighs — bare, brown thighs — and I looked up, farther still, and could see from my angle that this presence, this woman . . . was not wearing any underwear!"

Ignacio's eyes are insane and he leans back and now you are required to say something in response but your mind is a blank and there is a sound in your ears like the sucking of a vacuum, and so you say simply this: "Wow."

"That is nothing," he says. "Now I will really tell you something." He fans the air between you. "I was stunned by the sight of this woman's genitals. I was helpless, frozen, a blinded animal on the highway. And then there was the faintest shift in the breeze, and from where I was kneeling, I swear to you I could smell it . . . her *fresh . . . vagina!*"

With the utterance of these last two words you find yourself categorically lost and alone in the world, and if an earthquake suddenly ripped the bar in two you would raise your arms and invite a piece of the building to visit your skull and crush it to dust. Ignacio finishes his story (this presence was of course the little girl, now grown, returning to pay for the painting by offering her virginity, which he accepts, and he is a passionate and superhuman sexual machine and she is

a voracious whore, and then she is gone and he smokes a cigar in his bedroom alone) and you stand before him as long
as you can but your chin begins trembling and you feel you
have finally reached your limit, that your ears and heart cannot absorb any more of the regulars' filthy, detestable disinfor-
mation, and your eyes well up and Ignacio, concerned, asks
you what's the matter and you push past him apologizing and
rush out the door and into the alley, surprised to find that you
are openly crying. Once this starts you believe you will not be
able to stop, or will soon reach a point from which you will
not return without damaging your mind, and so to put an end
to this falling feeling you draw back your hand and punch the
brick wall as hard as you can. Now your hand is like a frozen
claw, and you reenter the bar to show Simon the blood and
shredded skin and are sent home and in the morning your
hand is twice its normal size and you realize through the fog
of pain that your wife is gone, the closets and bathroom cup-
boards bare. On the pillow a note.

# Two

Dana is eighteen and gains admittance to the bar with her stepmother's ID card. Her stepmother is fifty-two years old. You are thirty-two. Dana's boyfriend, Joey, is twenty-seven. They sit together and laugh at you as you approach—they are small and brown-skinned and find something comical about your tall and skinny white person. You like them both very much and give them free drinks and they never once tip you but this is not due to any cheapness of heart but a lack of tipping money. Not that they would tip extravagantly if they ever won a large cash prize. They have never been and will never be flashy, money-throwing people, and this is fine with you because their eyes are genuine and they like you and you imagine them doing imitations of you when they are alone, hiccupping, struggling with gravity, and adjusting invisible eyeglasses.

There is a scandal attached to their romance, and this is what it is: Joey had been Dana's gym teacher. Their relationship was uncovered by the high school vice principal, an ambitious man with adult acne, intensely disliked by students and faculty alike. He one night found Dana and Joey holding hands and kissing at the local pizzeria and did not intervene but alerted the news media, who descended on the restaurant with their camera lights blazing and microphones pointed lance-like toward Joey, at that moment entertaining Dana by chugging Bud Light from a frosted glass pitcher. He was humiliated publicly and dispatched "with a flamethrower"; Dana was beaten by her father and suspended indefinitely. The vice principal was promoted and threw himself a party in the cafeteria and nobody, not one person with either professional or personal ties to the man, came.

But now Dana has taken her GED and the unfortunate tale is behind her. She lives alone in Culver City and works two part-time jobs and is happy enough with her life and with Joey but her youth will not allow her true contentment and as the months pass she turns an eye to you. Joey leaves town overnight for an interview at an all-girls Catholic school in San Francisco and Dana arrives alone at the bar, drunk, in a low-cut blouse. She stays after hours and takes off the blouse and her skin is flawless and everything is all over in a matter of three or four minutes and you and she sit side by side staring into the darkness of the back room, the smoke from your cigarettes drawn into the space and disappearing. You think you can hear her crying but you do not want to look over or ask her any questions or try in any way to comfort her and if she got up and ran out the door you would not stop her. "I've never been with a white guy before," she says, extending a chubby baby hand, your pants still gathered at your ankles.

Discuss ginny with her short brown hair, her pug nose, and her plump red hands like spotted meat left to swell in the desert sun. Her eyes are popped and her pores emit a smell of chili dogs and french fries dipped in mayonnaise and you cannot help but wonder what horrors reside in her large intestine. She actively attends both AA and NA meetings but is always the last to leave the bar and will often stay after hours, by which time you are helplessly drunk and accordingly interested in her large white backside. She follows you into the storage room and will partially disrobe to be fondled and lightly slapped but she always stops you short of achieving anything purposeful and she will never touch you but only be touched. Now she puts her clothes back on and is very red and she leaves the bar with her hair in a mess, smiling in twisted triumph at the thought of your unfulfilled and piggish desires, and you curse her and her teasing ways, for after all she has done this before, to you and others, and you tell yourself this will not under any circumstances happen again. It happens again and again and again and again.

DISCUSS DANIELLE. She is fifty-six, with brittle, overdyed burgundy hair and orange lipstick and many sad tattoos whose meanings she hopes to share with you. She is a friendly person but has a greedy little girl's heart and her eyes grow narrow as she drinks and she looks at you as if you were the last piece of cake at the party. Margarita salt is gathered at the corners of her mouth and you sometimes walk with her to the storage room but only if you are extremely drunk. (She is forever buying drinks and placing them before you and calls you a spoilsport if you demur.) There is an honest light in the storage room and you want to smash it out to put Danielle at ease but she does not appear to mind, despite the bad times imprinted on her face and the shadows that dance beneath her bangs and eye sockets as she leans and then lunges toward you. You are backed against the ice machine and the storage room is spilling over and you want to scream and laugh and shout and punch Danielle in her gut but she is working your belt like an angry parent and you know that you have come too far to turn back and so you stare at the bare bulb until it burns out your eyesight black and pulsing.

Discuss the short, overweight Hispanic woman who follows you into the storage room after you winked at her. She is so unattractive you believed this would be harmless but she has misinterpreted the gesture as one of lustful beckoning, and now without even a kiss to share she is on her knees, and though you are well behind in your work duties and have no time for such things you find your hand is reaching up to lock the deadbolt. You try to concentrate so as to expedite the romance and are staring at the labels of the many bottles on the shelves when the woman begins grunting and you assume she is doing something to herself as well as to you and you are looking down to see if this is true when you notice that her hair is so thin she could only be described as balding or partially bald, and your jaw drops at the corpse-gray color of her scalp and the dainty, pink-and-blue veins crisscrossing her head like a roadmap. You manage to finish up and the woman is standing and holding you around your torso. Now you can see her scalp plainly and you want to know if she has recently gone through some cancerous ordeal but cannot think of a way to bring this up without causing offense. You ask if she is all right and the woman looks up at you, the eyes of a stranger. She tells you she misses her boyfriend.

Discuss the alcoholic and narcotics-addicted pharmacist woman who you believe is actually a pre-op transsexual male. She is short and thin with an attractive, heavily made-up face and drugged bedroom eyes. Her short black hair is crunchy from hairspray and her bare shoulders are covered with tiny bumps that you assume are the result of whole-body shaving or waxing. She has a different man with her every night; he is always dark-skinned and hairy and a little unsure and frightened. These are lonely men and they come to hate you when they see that their date has feelings for you, and they ask her to leave for another night spot; when she will not go they leave alone and the woman shrugs and looks at you suggestively. She has asked you many times to walk her to her car or to the ladies' room, and has asked to accompany you to the storage room, but you always say no because there are certain mysteries in the human world that you have never been curious about and here is one of them. But one slow night you are so drunk and so completely uninterested in breathing and living that when another bartender dares you to find out once and for all the gender of this being, you lead her by the hand to the back bar men's room. Her eyes are wide with sex-craving as you walk her into the stall and you embrace her and begin to kiss her and you will know in a moment whether she is male or female when her bare leg touches the cold porcelain of the toilet and she pushes you abruptly back and storms out of the bathroom and toward the front bar. You follow and ask her what's wrong and she is nearly in tears and wants to know if you honestly believed she was the type to be groped beside a toilet? Just what kind of a whore do you think she is? You tell her that that was precisely what you were hoping to find out and she slaps your face and leaves the bar swinging her purse like a mace. There are five or six customers in the room and they are applauding the performance and you wave to them modestly and the bartender's face is set in inquiring stone.

THE SHAMMY IS SHAPED like a television set (her head is shaped like a toaster oven) but one night she draws you into the storage room with the aid of fishnet stockings and lipstick and whiskey and dim lighting and her sweet, truthful smile. Now she comes by every evening in hopes that the stars will once more shine in her favor, and this is very sad because she lives an hour away and takes public transportation to visit you, and because you are looking sickly and do not smell good and have not once said anything of consequence to her, and the idea that you are an inspiration in this girl's existence is a true life's tragedy.

She probably loves you but you ignore her because you will bring her nothing but heartache and you know that if you ever see her cry you will want to kill her out of pity. But when she enters the bar shaking and with ripped tights and tells you she was mauled on the bus you feel a kindness for her and tell her she can sleep at your place if she likes and take the bus back home in the morning, and this cheers her and soon she is drunk and beaming. Throughout the shift you tell her that there will be nothing sexual between you and that you are thinking only of her safety and comfort and she agrees completely but is telling whoever happens to sit beside her that she is going home with you tonight so that soon you are being teased by your coworkers and by the child actor and Curtis, who says, "You really bagged a babe this time, boy."

You drive to your home with The Shammy at your side.

You are once again operating the magical LTD. (When your wife left with the Toyota you were forced to clean and partially repair your old car. You had it towed to a shop, where the mechanic would neither confirm nor deny the vehicle's magical powers. When pressed, he admitted he was a Chevy man. He got the car running for under a hundred dollars and gave you a mesh-back hat free of charge.) You are very drunk and have to close one eye to see the road and The Shammy leans against you and coos and rests a hand on your lap and soon your resolution is forgotten and you wake up hours later to vomit and wonder at the broad, freckly body lying on what was once your marriage bed. The Shammy raises an arm, milky white and thick as your thigh, and tells you that she is starving and wonders where you will take her for breakfast before driving her home (you never said you would drive her home). She names a brightly lit restaurant frequented by acquaintances of yours and asks for the telephone and invites several friends to the restaurant as well. They have heard all about you, she says, and cannot wait to finally meet you.

MOLLY DRAWS YOU from the bar to an after-hours cocaine house party where you refuse the cocaine of the hosts and are asked to leave. You do not leave but retire to their backyard; spying a tree house you climb up the two-by-four ladder with a half-empty bottle of Jameson between your teeth. This chips the bottle and you enter the enclosed tree house pulling glass bits from your tongue and gums. There is blood on your fingertips, not too much, and the whiskey burns the little cuts in your mouth and Molly finds you sitting Indian style, wiping the blood on your pants. She takes off your pants and hers and there is no way to accomplish what she hopes to accomplish in so small a space without her head sticking out the glassless window, and so this is what she does. Your bodies are rippled with goose bumps and she is grunting and the light of the early morning is beginning to glow so that when you accidentally drool on her back you see your spittle is all blood and you imagine your teeth must be covered and smeared red, like a boxer, like a street fighter, like a man walking away from a senseless tragedy, and you grin and wish like a fool for a mirror and camera.

P EG LEANS YOU against the jukebox and rubs your midsection and whispers crude things in your ear but will not go into the storage room with you. After a particularly freespirited year when she slept with every male employee at the bar other than you she has vowed to reclaim her morals and will not have sex for thirty days, and has twenty days to go, and you wonder if she will make it. Her ride home abandons her and she is forced to stay after hours so that you can drive her but now she will not drink and she will not let you near her and there is a look in her eyes of mistrust and even fear, but she is not afraid of you, only herself. You imagine there was a particular incident that informed her to go celibate—an excess of drugs at a male-dominated party is your guess—but you have ceased caring about the misfortunes of others and can no longer remember whose troubles belong to whom and so you do not bother to ask anyone anything anymore. You offer to pay for Peg's cab fare but she says she prefers to ride with you, and you ask her if she is sure, and she says that she is, and she settles her bag on the bar and asks for a double whiskey, no ice, and you sadly serve her.

You are parked on Rossmore and the old-timey neon sign on the roof of her apartment building illuminates the exposed interior of the LTD and she is facing you and you are drunk but not terribly so and you curse yourself for not bringing along a bottle. Looking into each other's eyes and speaking together in low tones, it becomes apparent that she hopes you will walk her through her troubles and show her that male-female relations can be lovely even in loveless union. She is looking for lust fulfilled but she searches also for respect, and in this she is out of luck because you do not know her or like her very much and you do not respect yourself and so the most you can offer this girl is time out of her life and an unsatisfactory meeting of bodies and, if the fates are generous, a couple of laughs and good feelings. At any rate there will unquestionably be a divot in your hearts before dawn and Peg seems to pick up on this and after thirty minutes of groping and pawing (the car interior is growing damp with dew) she breaks away and with great exasperation says, "What do you think you're doing?" You are smiling, because it is an utterly stupid and boring question, and you say to her, "I am sitting in an American car, trying to make out in America," a piece of poetry that arouses something in her, and you both climb into the back seat for a meeting even less satisfactory than you feared it might be. Now she is crying and you are shivering and it is time to go home and if you had a watch you would snap your wrist to look meaningfully at it but she dabs at her face and says she wants you to come upstairs and share a special-occasion bottle of very old and expensive wine and as there is no way not to do this you follow her through the dusty lobby and into the lurching, diamond-gated elevator and into her cluttered apartment to scrutinize her furnishings and unread or improperly read paperbacks, and you wonder if there is anything more depressing than the habitats of young people, young and rudderless women in particular.

The wine is all sediment and the cork crumbles into the bottle and you sit at a yellow Formica table in the dingy kitchen of Peg, drinking the vinegary wine (she is picking out the cork pieces, you are chewing them) and hoping not to talk, but now she wants to talk, and to understand and suffer, and as a result become humane and wise. She leans in and is serious and meaningful and you know what question she will ask before she asks it, and then she asks it, and the asking is terrible:

"Why did your wife leave you?"

DISCUSS THE SISTERS Valerie and Lynn, who invite you and a regular named Toby to their apartment after hours. Toby is a quiet, drowsy young man who drinks warm gin with PBR chasers; he sees the girls to the bar exit with a promise to follow close behind and returns to clap and laugh about the probability of forthcoming nudity. He urges you to hurry with your cleanup but does not offer his help. He is waving the directions to their apartment in his hand and he asks which of the pair you like better and you say you don't care and will leave it up to him. He weighs the pros and cons of each, saying that the younger of the two, Lynn, is prettier and sweeter, a bring-home-to-mom type, but Valerie looks to be more immediate, vulgar fun. And while Lynn might look nicer on his arm, it would stand to reason that Valerie would be the more skilled behind closed doors. It is all very exciting for Toby, this choosing of women, and you enjoy seeing him so happy, and you wish that you too were happy, and you have another large drink knowing there will be no noticeable effect on your disposition and that it will only make you sicker the next morning and probably render you incapable of anything sexual that night. (There is no taste on your tongue and it is like you are swallowing gusts of hot air.)

The sisters' apartment is even filthier than you had imagined it would be (the bathroom is unspeakable). Valerie and Lynn are in transition from one trend-based lifestyle to another and there is a feeling of limbo, past and present fads and interests muddling their slang, clothes, and décor. They are both on cocaine and their chatter is confusing to follow but it appears their current hope is to find work as traveling burlesque dancers. Toby is all ears and interjects when the girls gasp for breath, offering his encouragement and complimenting the furnishings. "I think this is the most comfortable couch I've ever sat on," he tells them.

Throughout their speech the sisters have been disrobing, an article of clothing at a time, and they now stand before you wearing only their underwear bottoms and high heels. It is all Toby can do to keep himself composed and he jabs you with the point of his elbow with such force that you cry out in pain and the girls ask if it would be all right to run through their newest routine and Toby says sure, sure, of course, goddamn, and you say sure, and they dim the lights and put on some music and perform a surprisingly well-rehearsed 1950s-style dance number that involves much breast-spinning and has Toby in a near frenzy—he cannot hide and does not seem to want to hide the fact that he has a full erection. The girls are bent over and smiling at you from between their legs and Toby like a zombie crosses the room to slap their backsides and comment on the resulting jiggle of flesh and of the two it is the younger and prettier sister, Lynn, who responds to this treatment, and she leads Toby down the hall to her bedroom. Valerie stands and is panting, her hands on her hips, and she takes you into her room and turns off the lights and lays you on her bed, asking dirty sex questions that you are supposed to answer with dirty words of your own but you cannot get started and your head is burning with whiskey and cigarettes and when she takes off your pants and lays her cold hands on your body your pulse is still and nothing happens. She abandons this project and asks if you will do her a favor and then she describes the favor and there is no time to answer yes or no before she throws a leg over your face and you are forced into action, allotting her fifteen minutes of your life before pushing her off and walking pants-less to the bathroom to wash your face, and here your heart jumps when you see your reflection because you are covered in blood. Valerie walks in and does not apologize but says you look like a scared clown and laughs as she sits to urinate. You can hear Lynn down the hall in the throes of passion (it would seem Toby knows a trick or two) and Valerie watches you scrubbing the blood from your stubbly beard with her toothbrush. "I always get the dud," she says, standing and flushing, pink swirling water in the sink and toilet.

ONE NIGHT, DRUNK but steady, you decide you will not go immediately home but look into one of your proposed after-hours adventures. You do not suppose you will see it through but you are curious about it all the same and you bypass your neighborhood and head west on the 10 freeway, toward the ocean. There is a ways to go and you chain-smoke and drink whiskey from an emptied soda bottle as you drive. On the radio a man is imitating a chicken singing "In the Mood." You are imitating the man imitating the chicken and spilling whiskey down your shirt front as you choke and laugh.

You park your car opposite the Santa Monica pier and find it is not dark and deserted, as you hoped it would be. The fun rides are still lit up and in the distance two security officers, a male and a female, are leaning over the railing and talking. They are standing close together and the male is pointing out at the ocean; the woman is nodding. They are near the end of the pier and you cannot see their expressions but you believe they are smiling. It is a romantic enough scene but antagonistic to your plans, and you toss out the empty soda bottle and drive north, down the California Incline, toward Malibu. The console clock reads four in the morning.

The air is dry and warm and you find the Malibu pier deserted and dimly lit. You park the car and walk down the beach and beneath the pier. Small waves lap over the barnacled pylons and the pier lets off a long, settling moan and you reach out your hands to feel the vibration through the mossy wood. The pylons are tall as trees and seem to be leaning or falling toward one another. You bend down to touch the water and it is cold but not so cold as you thought it would be and you take off your shoes and wade in up to your ankles, feeling with your feet the hard sand of the ocean floor. As your skin acclimates to the water you know that you must see your plan through and it becomes in that instant a significant ambition and you clamber up the beach to the side of the pier and jump onto the railing and lift yourself over. You disrobe to your underwear and run twenty paces before coming to a tall white gate, its top arched and slick. Using the pier railing for support you climb around so that your body for a moment is hanging over the ocean. You run forty more paces and hit another fence, identical to the first, and you notice an elevated shack at the end of the pier. A light is glowing in one of the windows and you decide you have gone far enough. Once again you climb over the railing, only now you are facing the ocean. Looking down to gauge your height you find you cannot see the surface of the water and you search the sky for the moon, but the moon is not there. The warm wind runs off your torso and legs and your mind turns to the loveliness of narcotics and alcohol and women and you are shivering though you are not at all cold and you feel that you could cry now. You cannot see the water but the shore is a long ways off and you know it will be deep enough and so you count aloud, one, two, three, and you hold your breath and jump out into the night.

You ARE SITTING in your car outside the bar, drinking from an airplane bottle and smoking a cigarette. You are forty-five minutes late and there are three empty airplane bottles at your feet and you have been parked for over an hour but are not yet ready to go to work. You no longer push headlong into your shifts and it is becoming more and more difficult to enter this building and in fact it is a constant worry so that you wake up thinking of the colorless faces of the customers and the cold, wet dishrag that hangs from your belt loop and slaps at your leg. Also you are always fighting one illness or another or one endless illness that never entirely dies, as you do not give your body sufficient rest and respite from your appetites. Now your body tries to reject the airplane-bottle whiskey by vomiting but you better the body with deep, mechanical breathing of the fresh night air.

As you exit the LTD, Junior the crack addict sneaks up and lifts you off the ground in an embrace and roars in your ear that he is back, back, back, muthafuckas! He sets you down and you catch your breath from laughing. "I really thought you'd died," you tell him. "That little guy was going around saying he'd killed you." "Hey man, no muthafuckas killin' *me*," Junior says. He has been in jail for three months and was released just this morning. You ask him how it went and he bugs his eyes at the stupidity of the question. You ask why he was arrested and he bugs his eyes doubly and rests his fists on his hips. You give him twenty dollars and listen to him talk about his latest plans—forthcoming construction work, doorman work, and a management position in an as yet unopened jazz club. Where he got this last idea is anyone's guess but when he describes himself standing at the bar in a suit and fedora with alligator shoes and purple silk stockings you cannot help but believe in some part of it. It is now only a matter of months, he tells you, a matter of hanging on.

He is eager to return to his routine and judging by his looks has already indulged profoundly in his drug of choice. He intends to make up for lost time, he says, with ninety days of his life stolen away forever when he wouldn't hurt a soul in the world, and when every day is a gift from God. He tucks the twenty away and turns a critical eye on you. He has heard you are doing poorly and asks if he might help. He infers that your job is in jeopardy but will not name the source of this information. "You're getting too deep up in it," he says. "Why do you think they call 'em depressants? You ought to do like me, see?" He points to his eyes. "Stimulants. Stimulated." Thanking Junior for his concern and insights, and promising to return soon for a longer visit, you walk to the front door of the bar. "Stay positive," he says in parting.

The room is already full and tossing or listing as a vessel over rough waters. Simon, returned to the role of manager, catches your eye and makes a show of psychically mutilating your character from across the bar. (At first he had refused the offer to resume his previous duties but a bonus was offered, a trip to some desert resort, and he came back to work with an extreme sunburn/new attitude. You are happy that he is in command again; you felt a keen pity for him when he was demoted, to the point that you wished he might "be killed.") He throws a rag at your face and nods in the direction of the bathroom. "Clean it up," he says. He is very angry but you do not attempt any excuses or penitent greetings; you walk past the line and into the men's room where you find a large pile of excrement perched on the seat of the toilet. Though this is the personification of your work fears you do not so much as sigh but take up a handful of napkins and, holding your breath, pick up the pile to ease it into the clogged, near-overflowing toilet, only its weight is too terrible to consider and you drop it into the filthy water. This creates a splash and your thighs are covered and you inhale the smell and vomit straight away like a fire hose and it covers the toilet seat and tank and spreads across the floor. Simon is standing behind you. "You'll have to clean the puke up too, mate," he says. "That's just the way of it." The child actor is standing in the doorway laughing and calling to Curtis that he might also witness the scene. Now they are both laughing and holding their stomachs and Simon is sorry for you and pushes them back down the hall and asks you in a mournful tone to try to finish the job hastily as there is a backup of dirty glasses and after all it is Saturday night.

You mop up the vomit and head to the bar to wash the stacks of glasses, hoping to numb your active mind in this mindless work but find that you cannot. You move sideways toward the whiskey assortment but there is Simon, shaking his head. "Not tonight," he says. Half an hour later he steps away for a cigarette and you rush to pour out three pints of alcohol, two Jamesons and one well gin, and you take these to the end of the bar where the child actor and Curtis are sitting elbow to elbow. They are still laughing at you and you nod good-naturedly before presenting a pint to each of them and holding yours high and calling it a race whereby the loser pays. They are rippling from bad street cocaine and gulp hungrily at the glasses and in three minutes they have finished up, neck and neck. You have secretly emptied two-thirds of your whiskey into the trash can but point to the remainder and say the round is on you, and the child actor and Curtis cheer, and you drink what is left in the glass and return to work.

As you bus the room and drain the sinks and replace the limes and olives and ice and napkins and straws and liquor and juices you keep a close watch on Curtis and the child actor, for no amount of cocaine can overpower a pint of eighty-proof alcohol consumed in so short a time, and you are curious to see how the drinks will take them. At first there is no noticeable difference other than their sudden, shocked silence. Then the smiles drop from their faces and their heads look to have tripled in weight and their eyes lose all focus and the child actor reaches out for a glass of water that is not there. Ten minutes later Curtis falls from his stool and does not get up. The child actor is afraid and uses his last burst of energy to push through the crowd to the bathroom. As he rounds the corner you see vomit spray from his nose holes and Simon turns to you with the mop and says, "I'm afraid it just isn't your night." He is laughing and you should be too but you cannot laugh or smile anymore. Raymond looks up from his drawings and corrals you as you pass. He is drunk and he brings his little ruler to your forehead and drags its edge from your hairline to the bridge of your nose and says, "You are forgiven." You snatch the ruler away and whip it over Raymond's head and it fans across the room and hits an oblivious fat woman on her chin. Her male companion stands and bares his fists but he does not know where the ruler came from. The woman covers her face and starts to cry.

Heading down the hall a man asks if you are working and you point to the mop and bug your eyes at the question and he hands you a cellular phone he has found. This gives you an idea and you do not clean up the vomit but lock yourself into the storage room and call 911 to report your suspicion that there is a bomb set to explode on the premises of the bar. You give a detailed account of an overheard conversation between two swarthy, bearded men and before you are even off the phone you can hear the shrieks of the customers and the breaking of glasses as firemen rush through the bar to clear the room. You reach up for a bottle of Jameson and break the seal, taking a long drink and inhaling deeply from a cigarette. When the evacuation is completed you let yourself out of the storage room and the bar is empty, and you walk from one side to the other drinking the whiskey and smoking, and crying softly—you cannot tell if the reason is relief or sadness. You look for Curtis's body but it has been moved. On the bar where Raymond was sitting you find a half-crumpled drawing of an adolescent boy, shirtless and in cutoffs, with a penis like a lasso. He is whipping it over his head and looks very happy to be living. You stuff this into your pocket and walk to the men's room where you find the child actor in a ball beneath the sink. There is drool draining from the corner of his mouth and his eyes are open to slits but you cannot see his pupils, only the reddened whites, and his breath is indefinable and you stand and kick him hard in the stomach and he vomits a cupful of gin and bile. Wiping the tears from your face you set your whiskey bottle and cigarette on the sink countertop and stand back against the far bathroom wall and rush forward to kick him in the center of his moaning face.

# Three

Discuss the renting of a vehicle and your conversation with the pockmarked counter man about the cars he has to offer you and then about the cars he does not have to offer but that he wants to speak of anyway, foreign and luxury automobiles he hopes to someday sit in and drive around in and whose horns he would like to honk and whose powerful stereo systems would push air through his hair. Discuss his lewd innuendoes when you say you do not care for the color or make of the rental but only the size, as you plan to lie prone inside its walls. You make no visible response to the intimations, being medicated on fat white pills, with many more in an aspirin bottle stashed in your suitcase (you scattered a dozen aspirins atop the white pills as a diversionary tactic), and the counter man, understanding there will be no mannish banter, drops his head to tap chicken-like on his computer.

You select a truck with a shell or camper top and when the man asks for your destination you tell him you are driving to the Grand Canyon and he makes one last pass at friendship, asking for the purpose of your trip (he is typing and speaking at the same time, which impresses you), and as you have no real reason but only an elusive, mesmeric feeling for going, you tell him a lie, which is this: When you were twelve years old you visited the Grand Canyon with your mother and father and spent three happy days and nights in the area, camping out under the stars, burning hot dogs over a barbecue pit and watching them fall from the sticks into the fire, cursing, catching and killing lizards and snakes—all the wiles and whims of any fast-paced boyhood. Or this at least is what you have been told took place those years past because you cannot, inexplicably, remember a single thing about the vacation, not the canyon's alleged breathtaking scale or the mules that are said to carry camera-laden passengers the eight miles down a treacherous trail to the canyon's shaded floor, and you share your frustrations with the counter man, telling him how bothered you are that one of the world's wonders has been shuffled from your mind, and you tell him that at the end of the day you simply believe the Grand Canyon deserves another chance to make a proper, durable impression.

The counter man has ceased working and is looking into your eyes for signs of psychosis. He asks that you have a seat while his people bring the truck around and you do not sit but stand at a nearby brochure display to listen in as he speaks on the telephone with his regional manager and you hear him retelling your story of the Grand Canyon Forgotten with emphasis on the mutilation of blameless reptiles and he describes your crooked glasses and underarm sweat stains and you hear him call you a weirdo and then a real weirdo and he requests the authority to deny renting to you on the grounds of suspicious vehicular intent but the manager, either a sentimentalist or else a hater of snakes himself, is unconcerned by the story and the truck is brought around forthwith and the counter man is frustrated at his unsuccessful attempt to ruin your plans and does not wish you *bon voyage* but turns his dented head away to hate at the walls.

YOUR NEXT STOP after the rental office is the health food store, where you will stock up on supplies for the long desert journey. You have never been to a health food store before and are looking forward to the experience, this due more to narcotic euphoria than an interest in herbs or roots or any other healing elements. The rental truck is brand new and you fiddle with each knob and button and your feet feel as though they are bound in sable pelts, making for inelegant driving, but the sensation of movement is as pleasant as the quilted dreams of deepest sleep and you are not worried for your safety or the safety of your adopted vehicle, which you recall is insured from grille to tow knob, and you watch your feet rise and fall on the clean rubber pedals and experience a profound satisfaction at their activity.

Your trips to the health food store and the Grand Canyon were motivated by a visit with a liver specialist called Eloise, working from a strip-mall office in the dead-hilled community of Agoura, deep in the San Fernando Valley. She came recommended by the child actor, who called her Magic Fingers and said she could repair the bloodied organs of decrepit winos, but you were nervous about the visit because people often died around doctors and you had not seen one in years and the pain in your side had increased so that you sometimes doubled over in hissing pain.

Eloise was forty-five years old, with ornately decorated chopsticks crisscrossed through a bun of black and gray hair. She led you to the examination room and asked that you take off your clothes for your colonic and you froze and said, but I'm not having a colonic, and she slowly turned and her expression was severe and she said that just by looking at your eye coloring she could tell you were poisoned with alcohol and hepatitis and that there had to be a prompt and total change in your life or your liver would turn to charcoal and you would die, and that you had to begin treatment right away even though she did not have time for the procedure, and she made a stab at bedside humor, saying she would make time by eating her lunch throughout.

Her lecture frightened you—it was what you had been dreading, to the word—so much so that you surprised yourself by agreeing to the colonic, which was as you suspected it would be, humiliating and disgusting, and when she said you would have to go through this many times before your body was completely cleansed you wondered if death was not the more dignified route to take. Also you were shocked when you learned she had not been joking about her lunch: She put away a large bowl of rice with steamed eggplant and zucchini, all the while gesturing with her plastic fork at the running tube, alive with bouncing excrement.

You are thinking of all this as you walk from your truck to the health food store entrance. Eloise was unhappy when you canceled today's appointment (you called on a pay phone from the car rental agency) but when you told a lie about a family emergency she said she understood and that you were a good boy when you promised you would not think of drinking alcohol or taking drugs or aspirin during your absence. Wrenching a shopping cart free from the corral you decide you will not see her again and will try not to think of the colonic again and you will not tell anyone about the colonic and are glad to have ventured all the way to Agoura, where you will never in your life return and so never by chance bump into anyone who had seen you in the office, and you think of the stories you have heard of those who die only after they stop drinking and of the doctors who raise their hands up and say, "What a shame the man didn't come to me sooner." You decide Eloise is one of these, and feel a heavy burden lifted the moment you divorce yourself from her.

That you have wasted a portion of your pill-high thinking of such things as doctors and corkscrewed tubing is madness, and you strike them from your mind and relax your hands on the grip of the cart and stretch your neck to test your high and you feel that it is still with you and you enter the health food store and are contented to find it smells just as you hoped it would, like a giant, wheat-filled pill. There is soft music piped in from the ceiling and you browse the aisles for forty-five minutes, putting things in and taking them out of your cart and speaking with the store employees, telling them you contracted hepatitis C through a blood transfusion (lie) and are now in need of advice, and in their scrambling sympathy they refer to magazine articles and websites and they give you bottles of every sort, pills and muddy-looking juices, and also a pound of trail mix and a large container of blueberries, evidently a strong antioxidant. The manager offers to loan you a few books and she pulls these inspirational texts from a tasseled suede bag and fans them out on the counter for you to look over but you graciously decline and wish her a good morning and she responds in kind as do her coworkers, pimply, pretend hippies, tugging on their smocks and waving.

Sitting in your truck you open the bottles and take some of the good-for-you pills and then some more of your special white pills and you open a can of beer—you had stopped at a gas station and bought a single can of Budweiser—and stick this between your legs before setting out on your trip in earnest. There is traffic heading into but not away from the city and you stare at the disappointed faces stuck in their cars and lives and you feel the next wave of pills coming on and are certain you have made the prudent choice in planning this vacation and you drink your beer in one long gulp, breathing with your nostrils as you had been taught as a boy, with your eyes watching the road at a painful downward angle that makes you laugh (at the thought of the cricket-legged muscles on the backs of your eyeballs), and you toss the empty beer can out the window, or rather let go of it and it is sucked out the window (also funny), and you pull off the freeway to stop at a gas station for another can of beer and a phone card.

THE TRUTH IS that you had not planned to drink on this trip and in fact this was its grand if overly dramatic purpose: To travel and see the world without any alcohol and to think of what was broken in your life and wonder clearheaded about the mending of these broken things. This was the plan and it was a fine plan, only midway through your previous night of work you were offered the bottle of white pills at a price so low you were morally unable to turn it down. You took these pills home and thought to leave them untouched in the cupboard as a present for your homecoming when it occurred to you to bring a few along in case of any emergencies—certainly they would offset your desire for whiskey—and you were happy with your realistic point of view and you took four pills to celebrate this and also to test their strength and you were happy again to find the pills were stronger than you had hoped and when you entered gas station number one your only idea was to purchase a phone card but your high made you dull-minded and there you were in the aisles, looking and pretending not to look at the coolers and at last giving in and purchasing the one can of beer, and later when you realized you forgot to buy a phone card you stopped at another gas station and again you forgot the phone card (you remembered the beer) but took comfort in the thought of the next gas station, and you wondered where it would be, and would the cashier be friendly or unfriendly, and you felt an uncommon patriotic shiver as you considered the country's innumerable gas stations and markets and rest stops, small businesses thriving or going under, the owners gambling their very lives on customers like yourself, travelers in need of single cans of beer and forgettable phone cards, and you looked forward to the next gas station, gas station number three, and you drank your beer down so that you might meet up with it sooner.

TRAFFIC THICKENS IN Covina and you exit the freeway looking around for gas station number seven. You drive past an old bowling alley and decide to wait out rush hour at the bar, swearing to yourself you will not drink a drop of whiskey, and you say it aloud: "I will not drink a drop of whiskey at the bar in the old bowling alley in Covina." You do not drink any whiskey but you want to terribly and you pour out two more white pills and lay these on your curling tongue (you shudder at their taste and fill your cheeks with beer). Time passes, an hour, and when you do not feel the pills coming on you know there are too many blocking up your bloodstream and that by taking any more you are wasting them, and so for the time being you cancel them from your mind and focus instead on your surroundings.

You do not bowl and do not want to bowl but find the sound of bowling therapeutic and also the sound of the baseball game on the television, which you do not watch. You noticed seven or eight classic cars in the parking lot and it is easy enough to pick out their owners: Men and women in their sixties, bowling and drinking and talking; the men wear matching shirts and are members of some type of car or social club. A few of the women, old enough to be grandparents, are made up like bobbysoxers, with poodle skirts and ponytails. One is jumping and clapping at her husband's bowling ability, acting the part of the spry teenager. She is drunk, and follows her husband to the bar and asks in baby talk for a Long Island iced tea; when he refuses, she complains and you hear him say to her, "Goddamn it, Betty, if you don't settle down and shut your mouth up you'll be home with the cats next time we ride." The bartender winks at you and you look away, laughing into the flat of your palm.

Your right pants pocket is filled with blueberries that you eat with each sip of beer and a drunken woman at the bar is making fun of you, asking if you are eating grubs and potato bugs. "'M talking to *you*, Tarzan." She turns to the bartender. "The King of the Wild Bowlers," she says. You ignore her and she settles her tab and drifts away to the lunch counter and the bartender apologizes, saying in the woman's defense that her husband has recently died of "balls cancer" and that she is roughing it out these last few weeks. He brings you a beer on the house, and then another and another—he is drinking tequila shots but hides this fact from you don't know who; he initiates this apparent rule-breaking as a bonding point. Other than the occasional walk-up you are his only customer and he asks you friendly bartender things about your life and then he speaks about his and you tell a bad joke and he laughs too hard and lays a hand on yours as if for support and then strokes the top of your hand and winks again, and this wink is the wrong sort of wink and it makes you uncomfortable and you tell him to watch your drink while you step out for a cigarette and he balances a napkin on the beer can and you leave the bowling alley just as the social club erupts over some crucial bowling error. (Betty is sitting a lane away from her friends, arms crossed in frustration at a life passed too soon, and with too little excitement.) You try to sleep in your truck but owing to the heat and discomfort of the cab you cannot and so after stopping at a gas station for a beer, and again forgetting the phone card, you are shortly back on the 10 freeway, heading east toward the desert.

DISCUSS LAS VEGAS. It is eleven o'clock at night when you arrive. That you are here at all demonstrates ill will toward your goodwill trip intentions and eleven is a particularly dangerous time for someone struggling with whiskey jitters but as before you promise not to touch a drop and swear you will drink only beer and that you are stopping by only to wonder at the lights and also to duck into the piano bar at the Bellagio for their blue-cheese-stuffed olives, a personal favorite and rare treat.

You stumble climbing onto your barstool and the bartender—tall and leathery, his thinning hair bleached white and spiked for a ridiculous effect—dislikes you on sight. He looks to have been a cocaine addict in years past and is now the perennial desert bachelor. Sensing his disapproval and understanding the sensitivity of bartender-customer relations you do not ask for the olives right away but order a beer and tip extravagantly and he takes your money but gives no thanks and will not engage in any casino chitchat. You order another beer and throw more money at the man but can see he is steadfast in his opinions and so you go ahead and ask for a cup of olives as a side and he is glad to be turning you down when he tells you the specialty olives are not bar peanuts tossed around randomly but offered only when ordered alongside their top-shelf martinis. You tell him you had not meant to speak belittlingly of the olives and of course you will pay the cost of this special martini except you don't want to drink a martini but only eat the olives with your beer and the bartender cuts you off and says the olives as a house rule are not to be sold or given away as snacks and you cut the bartender off and loudly order a top-shelf martini with extra olives and no martini and the bartender is now truly unhappy and he brings you one olive and tells you to "eat the stinking thing and fuck off down the road," and walks to the end of the bar to regale a regular with this, his latest story: The drunk who really, really wanted some olives.

You are never angry and now you are angry and you do not know what to do about it. You want to attack the man but think with a shudder of your cellmates in a Las Vegas jail and so instead take four more white pills and hatch a revenge plan. You do not eat the olive. You squash it in a twenty-dollar bill that the bartender will have to clean before pocketing, and taking up a pen from your bag you write these words on a napkin:

> You are forty years old, a bartender in a bar in the desert. You hate the customers and the work but are trapped in the life as you have no other skills and have had no schooling or training of any kind. You have wasted your life drinking and doing drugs and sleeping beside women with hay for brains. You are alone and of no use to the world, save for this job, the job you hate, the job of getting people drunk. What will you be doing in five years? In ten years? There is no one who will look after you and you could die tomorrow and the only people who would care would be your bosses, and they would not be sad at your passing but only annoyed about having to interview new staff.
>
> Your hair looks impossibly stupid.

You place the folded twenty atop this note and walk away to hide behind a row of slot machines and watch the plot in action. The bartender picks up the money, peeling it open to find the olive, and raises his eyes to find you. He does not find you and you are proud of the revenge results so far and are preparing for the bartender's reaction to the napkin when he, without noticing the writing, balls it up and tosses it into the garbage. He drops the dirty twenty in his tip jar and resumes his work.

Your heart is broken; you sit there feeling it break. Your chin is trembling when a woman in tights and a bow tie taps your shoulder and points to her tray and asks what you want to drink and you say, double Irish whiskey no ice, and she walks off to fetch it and you, realizing what you have done, stand and leave the slots before she can return and you head for the exit and ask the valet how far it is to the Grand Canyon and he tells you, and you hand him too much money and drive quickly away from the shimmering, nightmarish town. (You try not to look but the casinos seem to be breathing, their glowing bellies expanding and contracting as you move past.)


YOU DO NOT DRIVE to the Grand Canyon but head north into Utah. There is no reason for this. Whiskey or no whiskey you are drunk and angry at yourself and you wonder why you are unable to help yourself and your mood is desperate and no pills will change this and so you take no more and you do not stop for single cans of Budweiser and by the time you pull over to sleep you are sick and in pain. You try and fish out four aspirin from the bottle but they have burrowed past the white pills to the bottom, and so you empty the bottle onto your lap and pick out the aspirin this way. You are parked in a truck stop fifty miles outside St. George, an expanse of dirt twice the size of a football field, and yours is the only civilian vehicle among the semi trucks. You gag down the aspirin before climbing into the airless shell of your truck and curling up with your blanket to sleep.

You do not sleep, or anyway you do not sleep well. There is an Indian casino opposite the truck stop that shoots from its rooftop exploding fireworks hourly, this in anticipation of the coming Fourth of July weekend. Also, the trucks that come and go throughout the night are forever settling and rattling and honking, and their horns are as loud as a ship's and you jump at the sound and rub your eyes raw and by dawn you have surpassed the pain caused by the drinking but feel you have become part stray dog, the touch of your skin like a bald and miserable animal. It is dry and hot out but you do not drink any alcohol. You enter the truck stop market and buy two bottles of water and drink these along with two handfuls of blueberries. Before getting back on the highway you put your wallet and pills into the shell so you will be forced to pull over before deviating from your original travel plan. You do not listen to the radio as you drive and you have no thoughts but rather a sound in your mind, or a weight, a gathering blackness. It holds your head to the side.

It is seven in the morning and you are just outside St. George when the bloody noses begin. You have not had a bloody nose since you were an adolescent and you are so tired that you do not notice anything at first but you touch your lips and come away with red fingertips and look down to find a line of blood drawn down your shirt front and soaking into the crotch of your pants. You stop in a diner and clean up in the bathroom, changing your shirt and washing your pants in the sink, as you did not bring a spare pair. You do not want to reenter the diner with a wet spot on the front of your pants so you dunk them entirely in water, wringing out the excess, so that they are now a uniform color and less likely to draw attention as long as no one touches you. You will not let anyone touch you.

You order a trucker's breakfast that you eat exactly one bite of. The waitress teases you about your lack of appetite and when your nose begins to bleed again she catches your chin with her dishrag before any blood can fall onto your clothes or plate. She is grateful for the departure from her routine and you hold the rag to your face and talk with her, making friends, and you ask her for a route through Zion National Park to the Grand Canyon and she writes down directions with a warning not to travel a particular highway that would take you through Colorado City and you ask her what's the matter with Colorado City and she says that's where all the "plygs" live and you ask her what a plyg is and she says, the polygamists.

"Don't you know about the polygamists?" She dips the rag in your water glass and dabs at the dried blood on your face. "Nastiest people I've ever met. The Mormons, or Latter-day Saints as they call themselves now, are changing with the times, but there's still a few of these holdouts with their caveman ways. They were getting nudged out bit by bit and got so fed up they ripped up their houses from the ground and had them transported across state lines into Arizona. They're a town on wheels now and they hate outsiders like hell. I went through there once but you won't catch me back again. They wouldn't have doused me with water if I'd been on fire, I don't think. I feel sorriest for the women. Can you imagine what they must go through in their lives?"

After settling your bill you purchase a map at the gas station next door to search out the quickest way to Colorado City and you are happy at this new adventure: The discovery of and visitation with the mean-hearted, exiled polygamists of northern Arizona. The day grows warmer and dryer and your bloody noses are coming more frequently but you are using your previously soiled shirt as a bib; the blood drips off your chin and you watch your gory reflection in the rear-view mirror and wipe yourself dry and eat more blueberries. You slap at your head and the steering wheel—you had meant to buy a phone card in the last gas station.

Dɪsᴄᴜss ᴄᴏʟᴏʀᴀᴅᴏ ᴄɪᴛʏ. It looks to be deserted and you are wondering if the polygamists have rolled away once more when you see from the highway a group of houses resting atop brick and wooden blocks. You turn off and park beside the village and are disheartened when you do not see anyone about, no faces in the windows or even an unfriendly rustling of curtains, and though you had planned to you are not brave enough to knock on a random door and ask for phony directions. You drive farther into town and come upon a string of roadside shops and park outside a churchy-looking thrift store. You walk the length of highway but each store is either closed or condemned and you turn back to your truck. When your nose begins to bleed you walk with your head held back, plugging your nostrils with your fingers, because you had not wanted to stroll around a strange town with a bloodstained shirt tucked in your collar. Now your nostrils are packed with clotted blood and your hands and the steering wheel are sticky and you have no water to clean yourself with and you drive ten miles down the road and are upset at having missed Zion National Park to look into a couple dusty windows and you wonder if you should call your waitress friend in St. George to bring her up to date. Hoping to wash up and have a cup of coffee you park outside what you think is a diner but turns out to be a social hall and you enter to find it is *full of celebrating polygamists.*

There are a hundred or more people in the hall, men, women, and children, and a hush blankets the room as you enter. Here is the reason for their empty homes and closed shops—a wedding, a funeral, a pre-Fourth bash, something. The children are barefoot and dirty, their faces hidden behind the long smocks of their mothers and sisters, women watching you with fear and revulsion. The men's sleeves are rolled up to the biceps, revealing a lifetime of labor and also tension caused by your presence; they look at one another and wonder what will be done with you. The party is separated by gender.

It is just as the waitress said—these people hate you and will not rest until you have gone, and you stand smiling dumbly in the doorway looking around for a coffee urn, and not finding one you call out, not to a particular person but to the polygamists as a body that you are looking to eat something, and is there a decent restaurant in the area? No one answers and in fact it is as though you have said nothing, as though they are looking not at a person at all but at the door standing open on its own, and the feeling of the group is, which one of us is going to close it?

You leave the social hall and return to your truck, continuing on until you hit a small post office where you park to write your wife a postcard (she is living with her mother in Connecticut). The wind whips through the cab and blood drips from your chin and drags across the card and here is what you write: "Beware the plygs of Colorado City, Arizona. They have no cups of coffee for the likes of you." The clerk in the post office is not a polygamist and she agrees when you say they could use a strong drink. "I treat them like they're ghosts," she tells you. "It's easier that way." You ask for a tissue to clean your nose and she fetches this along with a Dixie cup of tap water to wash off the dried, brown, flaking-off blood.

I⊤ IS FRIDAY, the third of July, and you are standing beside the truck with your hands clasped behind your back. The look and scope of the Grand Canyon is a world beyond anything you had imagined, anything seen in magazines or movies. The sky is gathering a deep red at the edges as the sun drops to the horizon and people line the lip of the canyon and none are speaking but only standing and watching. You look at their faces, sensing their amazement, and wonder why you do not feel similarly—for you the effect of the view is a distinct discomfort and uneasiness. You are dizzy from a strange rush of hot blood in your stomach and the closeness to something as fundamental as this canyon. You were not prepared to feel anything other than pedestrian amusement, and it weakens you in your spine and legs. Clutching your stomach through your shirt you say to yourself, There is too much of the earth missing here, and I just don't want to know about it.

A hundred-year-old lodge is connected to the parking lot and though you are still not hungry (you finished the last of the withering blueberries) you walk over to see about dinner, if only to get away from the canyon awhile, but the dining room is full and the hostess says you will have to wait an hour or more to be seated. She suggests you head over to the saloon to sit out the rush and tells you to drop her name for a free cocktail (at the word your face puckers and your neck recoils into your shoulders like a turtle and the hostess, raising her eyebrows, moves on to help the next customer). You still have not taken a pill or touched alcohol since you woke up this morning.

The sun has set. You pace past the saloon several times but do not enter and you tell yourself you will not unless delivered a sign informing you to, though you do not mean to wait for the hand of God to reach from the canyon and open the swinging doors but something more along the lines of catching sight of a pretty girl at the bar, or for someone coming or going to wish you a good evening. When no such thing happens you walk to the saloon doors to peer inside the darkened room and the bartender's eyes and the eyes of the customers turn to you and are shining wet like a raccoon's over a trash can, and you catch sight of the rows of glowing bottles and again feel the heat gathering in your stomach, only worse this time, as if blood is pumping outward from its pit, and you push away from the flashing black eyes and rush back to the truck, climb into the shell, and close the door at your feet.

You are panting in the windless quiet of the truck. There is something unmistakably wrong with your stomach, some new pain you have not yet experienced, and you search with your fingertips for its center. When the pain and heat do not subside you gag down four aspirin and lie back in hopes of sleeping but the burning discomfort will not allow it, and as it comes in sharper waves you listen to your own moaning and whining and this is the most wretched and lonely noise you have ever heard, and a sadness like a lead-weighted curtain drops and covers you and now, with no alcohol or narcotics to disguise the long-hidden emotion, it takes over your body.

Here is a force more powerful than yourself, a quickening black-crazy desperation hurrying into your bones, and you are frightened, as in the alley at work on the night your wife left, that you are damaging your brain, and you punch at the insides of the truck, except now the pain does nothing to pacify you but seems to intensify your desolation. You are flipping around fish-like in the shell, slamming your head on the wheel well hoping to knock yourself unconscious, and blood is streaming from your nose into your eyes and mouth when some recessed, rational part of your mind informs you that this is the purpose of your coming to the Grand Canyon, and so you let go of your body and allow the attacking pressure to smother its weight on you and you wrap your face in the blanket and scream through visions of the sadness of your wife and of the women at the bar and your life at the bar and the regulars at the bar and your life alone in the house where you once lived with your pretty wife but where you now cannot look out the windows, and you think of the loneliness of the murdered ghost in the bar and you scream and scream covered in the greasy blood and tears until your voice is blown out and you push only creaking air and do not recognize your own sound and your body in time exhausts itself, of both force and emotion, and you can no longer move and are merely shivering, and then you are settled, and still. You remove the blanket from your face. Your eyes are open and you are breathing.

A HALF HOUR of calm passes and you open the tailgate of the truck to bow your head at the wind. You wipe away the sweat and blood and grease with your blanket and look out at the moon hanging low over the canyon. Your body aches as after intense exercise and you feel a contentment, a kind of pride or sense of accomplishment, and think to walk to the canyon edge to study its blue-black nighttime coloring and you squat to exit the truck, taking the long step to the ground, and as your foot hits the earth your sphincter muscle involuntarily releases and two days' worth of blueberries and a good deal of blood blast down your pant legs running over your socks and shoes and gathering in a steaming puddle at your feet:

Silence.

I T IS NO SMALL FEAT to clean yourself but you go about it with the facility of a washerwoman, leaning over the sink of the nearby public bathroom and scrubbing your pants under hot water with a found flat stone wrapped in paper towels. You throw away your underwear and socks and stand naked from the waist down, stains running the length of your buttocks and legs, and you catch a piece of luck in that there is no one around to witness this scene. You put your wet pants and shoes back on and head for the saloon but it is just closing up, and when you ask the bartender for one shot of whiskey he declines. When you tell him you will pay double for a bottle he says, "I saw you give us that look over the doors earlier," and that is that. You take to the road.

Y OU DRIVE SOBER through Flagstaff, Sedona, and Jerome, settling in the early afternoon in Prescott, Arizona. There is a rodeo in town and the streets are overrun with horse trailers and street vendors and drunken desert people dancing and kicking up dirt. You check into a twenty-five-dollar motel and ask the woman behind the desk where the nearest bar is and she tells you about the section of town called Whiskey Row a half mile down the road. "Whiskey Row?" you say. She asks if you are traveling alone and when you say you are she warns you to be careful, because the rodeo can bring out a mean crowd and the local law enforcement is understaffed and generally uninterested. You thank her and she hands you your room key; it is bent and attached by a heavy chain and screw to an eight-inch block of particleboard. "People love stealing my keys," she explains. "I wonder if they put them in memento boxes or throw them out the window or what."

You walk straightaway to Whiskey Row, bulky key dangling from your pocket, and enter a bar and order a shot that you drink in a gulp. It hurts going down and your face contracts grotesquely and you fear you will vomit but you clutch at your throat to keep the shot in your body and the nausea soon passes. The bartender is an attractive female, roughly your age; she apologizes for staring and asks if you have ever tried whiskey before and you tell her you have not. Laughing, she asks how you're liking it so far and you tell her not very much but that you've heard it's an acquired taste, and you order another and she brings you this on the house before moving down to help another customer. The drink goes down smoothly enough and the bartender smiles when you order a third.

The bar is full of cowboys and their lizard-women and you listen to the scraping of their boots on the warped wooden floor and the sound of their voices carrying on, telling their stories, and you wonder, why does *everyone* have to lie? You are out of place here, an obvious stranger and city dweller, the recipient of dirty looks, but the cowboys are too busy assembling a quality drunk to bother with you, and anyway it is early in the day yet for purposeless violence, with the sun still out and ice cream-sticky children shrieking on the sidewalk.

The bar is filling up and the pretty bartender has little time to talk but after your fifth shot she knows you were lying when you said you never touched whiskey before and when she gets a moment's break she returns to you, her arms across her chest in simulated dismay, and you raise your hand repentantly and offer to buy her a drink so that you might make peace, but she says she cannot drink on shift and points to an antiquated rotating camera nailed to the ceiling above her head. You then ask when she gets off work and she tells you six o'clock, and you share with her your plan, just invented, which is this: You will retire to your hotel room to bathe and become handsome and at the end of her shift you will return and then, with her consent, the both of you will walk arm in arm to the rodeo, where you will whoop at the depressing, unfunny clowns and the tortured, hate-crazy bulls and the pathetic-loser lasso-artisans, and where you will drink without fear of probably broken cameras inside of which there is almost certainly no film, and afterward, more drinks, quiet drinks alone in a room somewhere with no one to interrupt you with their life lies and sour breath and weird, girly elf shoes, and then afterward, and afterward . . . and you trail off, and the pretty bartender smiles shyly and brings you another whiskey and pours herself a soda water and you touch glasses, and drink.

You apologize for rambling but she is smiling more and more now, and she admits she will be waiting for you at six, and she points to the stool she will be sitting on, and you in your happiness reach out to touch her hand and she takes up yours and her fingers are so soft and warm and your hearts are beating very fast when the barback, a quick, modestly pompadoured Mexican teenager, rushes up and whispers something in her ear and her spine grows stiff and all joy leaves her face and she drops your hand and walks to the far end of the bar to serve the impatient, thirsty cowboys. You are confused and ask the barback what just happened and he will not or cannot speak to you but as he wipes down the bar he motions with his head toward a large man drinking alone in the corner. The man is staring at you, and now you understand. Husband or boyfriend, he has some type of claim on the bartender and is displeased with your rapport, and you wonder, How long has he been watching? And did he see you looking each time she leaned over to fetch beers from inside the cooler? You raise your whiskey to him and drink but he only stares, and the stare is of an unmistakable sort: Soon he will walk over and insult and humiliate you by telling you to leave and if you do not leave he will drag you out with your hair in his fist and if you resist he will beat you into the dirt on the sidewalk and the dirt will be crunchy on your teeth and tongue, and the bartender will see all of this and you will hear her screams of mercy mixed in with the encouraging whoops of the cowboys and lizard-women and there will be no chance of victory or even a decent showing of spirit with so massive a man as this and so, with no other available option, you settle up your bill and stand to go. The large man watches you leaving but turns away as you reach the exit and you catch the gaze of the worried-looking bartender and hold six fingers in the air and she smiles imperceptibly and then, with the man now greeting an approaching acquaintance of his, she faces you directly, pushes her hair back behind her ears, and *winks at you*!

Now you are free on the street and you will not be beaten or forced to chew sidewalk dirt and you are more or less in love with the bartender and you cannot believe how crazy your heart really is and your pace quickens at the thought of your motel room, of rest and of cleanup, when you round the corner and something strange happens: You walk face-first *into a horse* hitched to a lamppost. He is an old, beaten horse with a scooped back and bare knees and fat flies cooling themselves on his eyes and he rears back at your touch but soon grows calm and leans into your hands as you reach up to stroke him. You have seen people in movies giving horses sugar cubes or other sweets and you search your pockets for mints or hard candies but find neither of these, only your white pills, and so you give the horse four, and then accounting for his weight, four more (he licks them off your palm, his tongue like a warm, living steak), and you watch him chew up these pills, his jawbone as long as your forearm, green-black flies still wading in his eyeball water, and feel a sudden compulsion to reach back and slap him hard on his gray cheeks and this is just what you do, you box this sleepy old horse's face for him (discuss, if you can, why you do this). Again he rears (the flies somehow hanging on) and you want very much to punch the animal in the face but you only yank down on his bridle and scream in his face the words "Bath time!" and you run like the devil to your room and all those you pass watch your dusty wake in hopes they will catch a glimpse of your pursuer and glean from his expression some motive for his fury.


THERE IS A MANTLE of dust covering everything in your room and a group of holes pockmark the wall above the headboard of the bed; seven holes, each punched with a small blunt tool from the inside out. You fill these with tissue paper, worrying as you work that you will find an evil eye hovering in the darkness. Standing back to look at your handiwork you say to the wall, "Wall, I have made you ridiculous." You draw yourself a bath, only you did not wash out the tub beforehand and are forced to drain it, clean it, and draw yourself another. You are very tired and fall asleep in the bathtub and when you wake up the water is cold and the clock radio says it is ten minutes to six and you remember the worn blue jeans and sleeveless T-shirt of the bartender and leap from the tub, slipping on the wet floor tiles as you dry yourself with the sandpapery towels.

You return to Whiskey Row to find the pretty bartender is gone. Her replacement rolls his eyes when you ask if she will be back—a common question, apparently—but when you say you had plans to meet her he nods and hands you a drink ticket upon which is written the word *Sorry.* "She must've liked you," he says. "Far as I know she's never been sorry before." You say nothing to this, but shrug. "Consider yourself lucky," he says. "Her man would've spilled your brains, and that's a fact." (You think of the sidewalk dirt clinging to your clammy brains and make a distasteful face.)

You order a beer with the drink ticket and move to the nearest open stool where you make friends with a lizard-woman named Lois, who tells you apropos of nothing that she is fifty-seven years old, and who hits your arm and calls you a dirty flirt when you ask her for the time. "Anybody can tell my watch is broken," she says, holding it up for you to see. "You don't have to make up lies to talk to me." You tell her you only wanted to know so that you would not be late for the rodeo and she becomes irate and says that you don't know a single thing about rodeos, and you agree, and she asks you not to talk to her about any rodeos, and you promise her you never will again, and she tells you that she's been around rodeos all her life and if you'd like she will accompany you to the rodeo and you tell her, thanks but no thank you, and she falls to glowering. When you offer her a drink she perks up and introduces you to her son, a man your age named Corey, sitting on the stool next to hers. He is dog-faced and dog-haired and has small eyes set very far apart and a baby-blond mustache growing *into* his mouth, and when Lois whispers in his ear he extends a hand to you and says, "Lo says you're buying drinks." You tell him you had planned on buying a few and he says a few would be fine, and he orders himself a shot of tequila and a Mexican beer and when given a price by the bartender he points not at you but to the wallet tucked in your hand.

Three rounds later they are desperate for you to stay. Lois grows adamant that you not go or anyway that you not go without her, and she holds your wrists and tells you the rodeo is "nothing but a heartbreaker" but refuses "on principle" to elaborate. Corey, less subtle than his mother, says, "I wish you'd stick around and buy me more tequila." But you are thinking of the bartender and you tear yourself away from the duo. Lois follows at your heels to the door and spins you around at the exit and says, "I used to be beautiful," and in the light you can see this is true, and you tell her she is beautiful now (she is not), and she smiles at you and asks coquettishly if you would like to be friends for life and you say, of course.

"You know about a spit shake?" she asks.

"No, Lois, I sure don't."

"They probably don't have it in the city, that's why you're all walking around with knives in your backs. But you've heard of blood brothers, haven't you? Well we can't do that one anymore because of AIDS and all, so out here we do a spit shake, and once you do a spit shake, you're loyal to the end. See, first you put a great wad of spit in your palm, and then me in mine, and we just grip our hands real tight and slippery—"

You cut Lois off before she can pack her fist with saliva, telling her you do not have time for the ritual just now as you are late to meet somebody, but that you will return after the rodeo and will be more than happy to oblige her then, and she is sad about your leaving but you tell her it is better this way, because now you will both have something to look forward to, and when you get back you can both spit all over each other if she would like, and she nods her head and reenters the bar, saying that she'll be around, and you'll know where to find her.

THE PRETTY BARTENDER is not waiting at the entrance of the rodeo and is not in the stands at the rodeo and is not at the concession booths and is not leaning against a fence with her arms crossed smiling at the exit of the rodeo. The rodeo is dull and hot and you cannot concentrate on its happenings, as busy as you are looking around and with the smell of the animals strong in your nostrils, gripping the pit of your stomach. Sitting behind you is a cowboy tapping repeatedly on your spine with the toe of his boot and apologizing; children are led away by their mothers to be put down in their beds and the eyes of drunken men that remain fall critically on you. The bartender has no plan of coming here. When the sun goes down the overhead lights snap on with a creaking, buzzing click and your hands look like an angel's hands floating before you in the glowing fluorescent whiteness.

Back at the bar you catch sight of Lois and Corey before they do you, and you push through the crowd to sit beside them. The room is at capacity now and there is a country-western band playing on a stage so high that as you pass by, the fiddler's boots are a foot above your head. Corey's little eyes meet yours and he points out your return to Lois, who swings around, waving entreatingly. Her head looks as though it has been taken off and put back on improperly—even without your money it is clear they have continued drinking in your absence. Lois works her elbow like a pump handle while summoning phlegm with a series of deep inhalations and you watch as she spits four times in her palm, and when you reach her she is beaming, holding the puddle of mucus out between you.

"All right," Corey says, "now you in yours."

You do not want to touch Lois's hand but can see no way out and so you spit once in your palm and hold it similarly outward. But this is not sufficient for a spit shake, neither the amount nor the ingredients, and you are informed to "get some glue in there," and you make a hacking sound with your throat and cough up a large ball of phlegm into your palm and clasp hands with Lois, whose spit runs over your knuckles and causes you to wretch so that you fear you will vomit, but you do not vomit and it is all over soon enough and Corey passes you both bar napkins and declares Lois and yourself Official and True Friends for Life.

"For Life," Lois says.

DRINKS AND MORE DRINKS, bought always with your money, and you find Lois's hand is resting on your thigh. Her thumb draws back and forth and Corey can see this and does not seem bothered but you are uncomfortable and try to involve him in the conversation. Lois drags her long, painted nails across your lap.

"Leave him alone," she says to you. "He's trying to make it with girls."

This is true. Corey's pickup method is to stare, with his little pig eyes, at the heads of unaccompanied women until they are made so uncomfortable that they ask him to stop; when he does not stop they collect their effects and move to another part of the bar, outside his field of vision. He does this again and again until there are only accompanied women within sight, and he drinks more tequila and begins looking at them, and they lean in to tell their cowboys and the room now turns to ugliness and the night begins its unraveling.

You are separated from your mind. Lois's hand is worming down the front of your pants and Corey is laughing and licking his mustache and you drink whiskey after whiskey and are taking pills now as well and Lois sees this and says, you don't know nothing about pills, and she hands you a baby-blue circular pill that you eat and which Lois begins immediately rooting around for, forgetting she has given it to you, and she empties her bag on the bar (you spy a roll of condoms) and says, that pill was just deadly, that pill was deadly and I lost it, and you give her two of your white pills and she orders two more tequilas, one for Corey and one for herself, and she gives her son a pill and he takes this without looking at it and *chews it up,* followed by the tequila, and you hear a cowboy tell him to stop looking at his wife, and Corey, having given up any hopes of finding love on this night, crosses over to fight the man, who stands and grips the neck of his beer bottle in his hand.

Lois does not stay to watch her son in battle but steals you away to the back of the bar and leads you to the darkened dead end of a service hallway. She is on you now, her gaping mouth breathing hot and foul-smelling air on you, and she places your hands on her body and yanks at your belt and zipper, and finding your body unmoved, begins whining and clawing your chest and humping your leg and she tries putting your hands up her skirt and inside of her but you drop them to your sides and your head lolls back and you are laughing, knocking your skull into the damp and sticky wall. She is in a frenzy and drops to her knees and you watch her head moving frantically back and forth and at the other end of the hallway you see the silhouettes of cowboys and you hear their shouts and wonder if they are watching your romance or the fight with Corey, and then you see Corey walking down the hall toward you and you smile at him and say, "Happy Fourth of July, Corey," and he has blood smeared on his cheek and he draws back and hits you in the eye and you drop to the floor and through your covered face see him drag his mother away by the arm like a rag doll.

YOU CORRECT YOURSELF and stand and return to the bar. Lois and Corey have moved to another table and neither will look at you and you are no longer friends. You try to buy the man next to you a drink but he politely declines, handing you a napkin for your bloody eye. "But you're sure you don't want something?" you say. "I'm sure of it," he says, then orders a drink and pays with his own money. The lights come up and the country-western band says goodnight and the bartender will no longer serve you and he points to the door and you file out with the others, speaking to those on your left and right and people smile and slap your back patronizingly but will not respond properly to any of the things you say.

All of the bars on Whiskey Row have closed and the street is overrun with drunks. Discuss the cowboy that is lifted up and carried the length of the street on the crowd's shoulders— here is the winner of the rodeo. He is just a boy, not yet twenty years old by the looks of him, and his smile is the truest and most handsome smile you have ever seen, and he looks sober and embarrassed at the fuss, but beneath this is an unqualified joy and pride and it is a living dream for him as he raises his hat and tosses it to the crowd, and you see the dagger hands of lizard-women reaching up to take pieces of him as he passes by.

The sight of the rodeo champion makes you sad in your heart and you decide you will visit your old horse and maybe steal him and ride him into the desert, but to do this you have to backtrack against the flow of the crowd and you are shoved and kicked at and offensive to those who touch you, and women gasp as you pass and recoil as you draw near, because your drunken blood is dripping freely from your eyebrow and your eyes are wet with tears, and some of the men you push past want to knock you down but are so repelled by the sight of you they move on or their women pull them along. But now you trip or else someone hits you from behind and you fall to your knees and a pair of hands are on you and they drag you to the side of the road and drop you there, and you are lying down in the dirt watching the boots file past, hundreds of pairs of cowboy boots, no two alike, walking along together in a pack.

The crowd thins out and you sit up against a hitching post and across the way you see the Mexican barback and call out to him and he walks over. He has a date on his arm and he asks if you are all right and you do not speak but give him the okay sign. His date asks him a question in Spanish and he answers in English, "This is the guy I told you about, the one that almost got it from Penny's boyfriend," and she nods. Now Penny the pretty bartender and her boyfriend come over to say hello to the barback and they see you on the ground and Penny gasps, and the barback asks her boyfriend if he is the one who did this to you, and he promises it wasn't and he reaches down and picks you up to stand and it is unusual to have his strong hands on you because he only wants to help you now, and he asks where you are staying and you point towards the horse and they as a group walk you in this direction. Penny cleans your face with a tissue and asks you what happened, and who did this to you, but you cannot remember just then and you say you don't know. Her boyfriend and the barback are holding you up and the barback's date says something in Spanish that causes him to laugh and Penny asks him to translate, and he does: "She says he walks like a cigarette thrown out of a car on the highway. You know, the way the cherry dances?" and they suppress their laughter at the girl's joke. You break away and they do not follow after but call to you, apologizing, and you hear Penny's boyfriend saying, "Let him go, let him go if he wants to go," and you stagger closer to the old horse, thinking of him standing in the alley by himself with nothing in his mind but gray sound and all of a sudden you are so sorry for hitting him like that, and you cannot understand why you would do such a thing and it seems to be the worst thing you have ever done in your life, and you choke and cry at this and have never felt so intense a hatred for someone as for yourself at this moment, and you will not ride the horse but stroke his face and make friends with him and you will give him more pills, all the pills you have to help him with his life's pain, and he will not know why but he will feel a supreme happiness and a change in the sound of his mind to a kind of heavenly and eternal music, and when at last you reach the alley there is goodness and repentance in your ringing spine and ringing heart but this vanishes when you find that the alley is dark and the tired old horse is gone.

# Four

Discuss your wife. It is the early afternoon and you are sleeping on the couch in the living room when she returns for the remainder of her things. She is packed and loaded and she wakes you up to speak with you. You are *down on your luck* but will surely *pull yourself up by your bootstraps* and afterward *come out swinging.* Now she looks at you and is thinking about her lost and probably wasted time and she becomes angry. Time is more important to young women than to men, she explains; this makes sense and you agree that it makes sense and you excuse yourself to vomit and though she does not know you are silently vomiting you are annoyed that so little has changed since she left you, because after all it would have been an exceptional feeling for her to come back and to see you dressed in clean clothes, with your hair combed and your glasses shining brightly, your shoes creaking with unbendable leather newness. Your wife is on the phone and you hear her tell someone she loves him or her and when she hangs up you say, who was that, who do you love? "I love lots of people," she tells you. "Who do *you* love?" When you do not answer she moves toward the door. A male voice calls out; you hear the honking of a car horn. "Who's that?" you ask.

"No more questions," she says.

"One more question," you say.

She stands there waiting for the question. But it is a cruel question and you shrug it off. She points to her watch and holds her palms out; you nod and point to the door and she is gone. Your telephone rings and you walk to your room to answer it. Your bed is made and the covers are cool and you bury your face in them, pulling the receiver to your ear. It is Simon calling from the bar and you say to him, good day, proud South African.

"Look buddy, are you on or off tonight?" he asks.

"What do you mean?" you say. "What's the matter?"

He says that he is tired of fielding calls from you when you are drunk and you say, what? He says that he has better things to do on a busy Saturday night at work than to listen to your abuse and you say, wait, what? He tells you that this last call makes the fourth time you have called the bar drunk and quit, and you begin to laugh and so does Simon, reluctantly. You explain or try to explain that you have been on the road and contracted a case of dreaded desert fever, and you ask is he aware that the symptoms of said disease include animal cruelty, sticky-wrinkly romance, and muddy drawers? He informs you that that is none of his business and he becomes angry again and reminds you that your job is to wash dishes, the work of an ape, and can't you do the work of an ape? And aren't you paid well enough, in cash? If you can't do it, he tells you, if you can't do this brainless work of an ape, there's a line of people waiting to do it for you, which is true and you know it is true and you, recalling your overdrawn bank account and upcoming rent, make a sincere apology to Simon and tell him you will shape up, not ship out, and he tells you he hopes so because after all, over the years he has grown sort of fond of you. You have three hours more to rest before leaving to open the bar and you are impressed with this length of time for it is somehow both too long to wait and also not nearly long enough.

Y̲OU ARE SITTING in the magical Ford outside the bar when Junior the crack addict walks up and steps into the car and you both sit there watching the building. His smell is otherworldly, like a demon from deep in the earth's crust, and he repeatedly passes the fiercest gas; he has been too long without his drugs and his body is causing a fuss. He does not greet you and you do not greet him; a rift has grown between you recently, or rather a rift has grown between Junior and everyone—he is in the worst way and the doormen say he has been robbing people with his machete blade after hours. You are not afraid of him and you do not believe he would ever do you any harm but you wish he were somewhere other than sitting at your side, wondering about the contents of your pockets.

He is fidgeting with a lighter and finally he says to you, "I need twenty dollars, man. I need it bad." When you tell him you haven't got any money he punches your dashboard and pouts, asking himself how long this torture might go on. You tell him to wait a minute and you enter the empty bar, retrieving twenty dollars from the safe. You walk it out to him and he is relieved to see this money but wants to know where it came from. When you tell him you stole it he looks worried and asks if you won't get into trouble, which is insulting because you know he does not actually care one way or the other. "Do your drugs or don't do your drugs," you say. "Don't stand around sobbing and bitching about it." He straightens himself up and nods and hustles off to find his dealer. All through the night you are bothered by guilt and self-loathing for speaking with him so harshly and angered that such a man could conjure these emotions in you.

Discuss your feeling of wonder when the pilfered twenty dollars is not reported missing at the end of the night. Discuss your routine of thieving that stems from this incident, and the criminal spree you quickly embark upon.

Your plan is to keep an at-home stolen-monies pile, separate from your life-monies pile, and to cultivate it to a respectable size and then, at some key point, utilize it dramatically. Within a month you have three hundred dollars and you feel great relief and satisfaction, as if justice has been served, and you wonder why you waited until this late date to begin stealing from the owner, who you (on a whim) decide is a bad man who expects you to gladly damage your mind and body with this potentially deadly work of washing dishes in a bar, and who has never asked you how your feelings were doing even though it is fairly obvious that they, your feelings, have been hurt and are still hurting yet.

But the pile of pilfered monies is not growing fast enough and you concoct another manner to steal from the bar and here is what it is: You do not take any money from the safe. For three hours during every shift you are alone in the bar, from six o'clock to nine o'clock each night; this is your time to shine. Two customers come in and order two beers and two shots and you charge them twenty dollars and you open the cash register (with its loud, clanging, official-sounding ring) but you do not enter the cost of the drinks into the machine and when these customers leave you retrieve the twenty-dollar bill and fold it into your wallet. When more customers arrive you repeat this routine and the next morning you count a hundred and twenty dollars to add to the pile. (There had been a moment at the end of the night, with Simon examining the register tape, when you were prepared to raise your hands and call the police on yourself, but he had said nothing and in fact had given you an extra twenty dollars because, he had told you, you actually seemed half sober for most of the shift.)

The strange thing is that from the time you began to steal, you *have* been drinking less. One reason for this is that you are fearful of being caught and wish to keep your head clear, but also there is something about knowing you are exacting revenge on those who have saddled you with this work life which has a calming effect on your entire attitude, and you are surprised to find that you are once again drinking not to black out your mind and feelings but for the old-time reasons of good-natured happiness and the desire to celebrate the rhythm of your own beating heart. And so you are faced with another of life's semi-annoying ironies: You were never such an efficient employee until you began to rob from your place of work. Now you are stealing an average of two hundred dollars per night, and your pilfered-monies pile is spilling over onto the floor. You purchase a chalkboard and hang it above the pile; across its face you write out things like: *Sailboat? European Relocation? Motor Home + American Road Odyssey?* These ideas and others rush you along in your life and you feel for the first time in years that you are living toward something of significance. Your wife calls to ask if you are doing any better and you say, if I were doing any better I'd explode, which she misinterprets as another one of your declarations of desperation, and she hangs up on you.

One night, overly confident and gladdened by your plans, you lose your sense of propriety and steal three hundred and fifty dollars over the course of your shift. This proves to be too much, and at closeout Simon asks you questions that lead you to believe he suspects you of thievery (he makes no outright accusations but his opinion lingers in his every word).

The next night you are setting up the bar when an exceedingly friendly man enters and orders a beer. He matches the tip with the beer cost and you, standing at the register, watch him watch you in the mirror above the bar and it occurs to you that this man could be a plant sent by Simon or the owners to uncover your fingers as either sticky or unsticky, once and for all, heaven help us, God bless us, may we rest in peace through eternity and the chilly outer reaches of space and time, so called (gavel slam). But Simon (or whoever) sent a man with poor eyesight and his squint gives him away definitively because there is no reason in the world for a customer to scrutinize your work this closely, so you, understanding your position, ring the order in properly, giving the register a wide berth so as to reveal the numbers of the transaction in neon, which the man sees despite vision problems. You hand him his change and he is acting the part of the glad beer drinker to your convivial, glad-to-be-here host. It occurs to you with a kind of wincing sadness that he is most likely an aspiring film star, and that this real-life role he is playing is his way of putting his skills to the test, and you can hear him saying to his bored-to-tears girlfriend or boyfriend, "If I can fool this bartender, I'll know that I've finally made it."

It is seven o'clock and a group of Hollywood types enters to celebrate the wrapping of a television commercial. They are throwing money at you hand over fist but the glad beer drinker still sits at the bar and watches your every move and you are becoming more and more annoyed by his presence when you think of your pilfered-monies pile, presently at a standstill. Hoping to get him drunk, you elect to switch him from beer to whiskey, offering him shots on the house, which he finds interesting, asking if you often give out free alcohol to strangers. You tell him, "No, there's just something so *real* about you, you know? From the moment I saw you I thought,

There's a regular guy." The glad beer drinker is happy to hear this and he accepts the whiskey in his hand and thinks of the time in the hopefully-not-that-far-away future when he will be interviewed and asked about his years of struggle and toil— this story of fooling a thieving bartender would make a fine, humorous footnote. You give him another shot, and another and another, matching shots with him and egging him on, only the glad beer drinker is no drinker at all and soon he is rubbing his eyes and cursing aloud to himself and he does not notice when you put a Post-it over the display on the cash register to cover up its telling numbers.

The crowd swells and you no longer ring in the drinks but only open the machine for the change, keeping track of the amount coming in on a piece of scrap paper. You give the glad beer drinker a fifth shot and he begins talking about a play he is in, and he asks do you have any idea how taxing it is to have to cry every night? He tells you that if you write down your name he will put you on the ten-percent-off list, and you thank him. Now Brent the unhappy doorman comes over and you point out the glad beer drinker as a drunkard with covert plans to upset the serenity of the room. Brent nods and takes the glad beer drinker by the arm and tells him it's time to go now, champ. The glad beer drinker is confused and begins to shout that you don't understand who he is, and that you're all going to hear about this later, that it's going to be your jobs when he gets through with you, and Brent bends the man's arm back in a painful hold and the man submits with a yelp and the crowd celebrating their television commercial cheer the glad beer drinker on, taunting him and calling out into the black and flashing room, and the moment Brent leads the man out the door you pick up a calculator and add up the pilfered monies and this number impresses you and you wolf-whistle as you fold the bills away in your wallet.

Dᵢscuss the later happenings of Curtis. He once was lost and in fact had been missing but now is found, and he enters the half-filled bar in regular civilian's clothes, and you can tell by the bobbing of his head that he has been drinking elsewhere. He marches past the tables and stands rigidly before you, saluting and announcing loudly that Private Curtis is reporting for duty, sir! And you, thinking that Curtis has at last done something humorous, move to pour him a whiskey which he drinks in a gulp before repeating the salute, etc., and you say, "Okay, little less funny the second time," and he explains that he is not making a joke but that he has *joined the Marines*. You ask him if he is aware there is a war on and he says that he is, and that he will sleep well knowing that he's done his part, a phrase that makes you want to drown him, and you tell him that if he's joined the Marines during the bloody reign of the present-day commander in chief he'll quite possibly wind up sleeping a little too well, which he seems to think is in bad taste, and here is something new: Curtis is offended by *your* vulgarity. Hoping to mend fences, you tell him it's free drinks till closing time, and you wish him luck with every passing shot and he drinks the whiskey but continues to sulk at your insensitive remark. Finally you tickle him under his sickening, gobbly chin and tell him that everything is going to be all right, which is a lie, and which he knows is a lie of the highest order.

It's free drinks till closing time but Curtis passes out hours before that. The child actor comes by to pick him up and you greet him like an old friend (you do not know why you do this). You remember the last time you saw him, when the bar was raided and you gave him a kicking; the child actor does not know exactly what happened that night or who it was that bashed his face but he is aware on a base level that you acted in one unkind way or another—his reception to your hellos is chilly and distant and when you tell him how good it is to see him he merely belches. Now he is struggling to remove the body of Curtis from the room; you are watching him struggle; Simon is standing at your side. Simon served in the South African military as a youth and he shares with you his doubts regarding Curtis's assimilation into the war machine. As you watch Curtis's feet disappear out the door, Simon turns to you and says, "That poor bastard doesn't know what he's in for."

"I hope he dies out there," you say, and you laugh-sputter at the statement because it is a terrible thing to have said aloud and you hope you can play it off as a joke but Simon is staring hard at you, and now he knows for a fact something he has suspected for years, which is that you have a streak of hate in your heart and that it is deep and wide and though you have hidden it, it is unmistakably uncovered now, and he will never feel that previously mentioned fondness for you again, and you can see the words in his eyes as plain as day: I'm going to get you fired from here, mate.

CURTIS IS GONE for five weeks (the child actor is gone for five weeks) but they return together to celebrate his, their return. You learn that Curtis did not go far in the Marines, was in fact kicked out of basic training because he could not shoot straight. "There's something wrong with my eyes. They tell me to shoot sideways," he says. He shrugs and clutches the whiskey you have brought him and when you ask how his feelings are doing he says the same thing he always says about those who reject him: "Fuck 'em in the ass." But you can see that his feelings are hurt and you wonder at the pain of a man stupid enough to be turned away from the Marines during a war.

The child actor has now clearly made up his mind about you and seems to have poisoned Curtis's mind as well, and you have never been so surprised as when they take out their wallets to pay for their drinks. They fan out their cash anticipatorily and it seems to you that the world is running backward and you push the money away but they insist on paying and Curtis, looking at you as though you were his oppressor, says, "No more. From here on, we buy our drinks." "Okay," you say in a you-asked-for-it tone of voice, and you tell them the cost of the round and they cannot hide their shock, for it has been so long since they paid for a drink they have forgotten the value of good Irish whiskey and imported beer. They pool their cash and pay out the round (no tip) but you notice that for the next, which they order from Simon, they ask for Pabst in a can and whiskey from the well, and you walk over just in time to cheers them, only you are drinking Jameson, and it is golden blond in the cup whereas theirs looks and smells like dirty gasoline. And you watch their quivering throats as they toss the whiskies back and you can see that their bodies wish to reject the foul liquid but they push the alcohol down into their stomachs and look at each other and shrug.

"It's bad but not that bad," the child actor says.

"It's bad but I've had worse," Curtis agrees.

You drink your Jameson down and your body welcomes it as though it were sunshine in a glass. Curtis and the child actor look at you but do not talk to you; they move down the bar to sit nearer Simon and you notice throughout the night that when these three speak they speak closely, in private, and that their eyes often fall on you: Three people who once liked you, who do not like you any longer.

Dıscuss your wife. She will not return your phone calls and has moved to Pasadena to live with and be closer to another man. You are at the bar, staring at the telephone and disliking it when Merlin enters for the first time since the party/orgy/bloodbath at Simon's house. The right side of his face is scabbed and he looks to be half starved and you are gladdened by his poor appearance because you have recently had many unpleasant dreams about him and have come to intensely dislike or hate him, and you wonder if he is addicted to drugs or living in his car or has contracted a fatal disease or fallen under the angry spell of a fellow witch-peer? He notices your happy and curious expression and is offended by it; he stands before you, resting his hands on the bar, and says after catching his breath, "You keep thinking about her but she isn't thinking about you. She's glad she isn't thinking about you. You weren't good for her life. Get on with your life. She'll never think about you again if she can manage it." He is exhausted by carrying the burden of these words and he walks heavily to the door, muttering to himself about a need for sleep and relaxation.

You are hurt by these words and you want to slash Merlin's face with a knife for saying them but he is gone and now there is nothing to do but live with them. You call your wife's new phone number and your heart sinks at the sound of another man's voice on the machine, with your wife laughing in the background at his humorous leave-us-a-message comedy routine. You hang up the phone and move to the whiskey assortment and take a short drink of Jameson (you are averaging a mere three or four short drinks per night now) but the taste is so terrible it makes you gag, and you cannot understand it because this has never happened to you before and you look at the bottle and say to its green-glass shoulders, bare and ladylike, "Not you too?"

You hear scuffling and shouting outside and you exit the bar to find Merlin being taken away in a police car; he is looking straight ahead and does not appear to be bothered or surprised by this. Junior is standing at the curb watching the squad car pull into traffic. You approach him and ask what happened and he tells you, "M-m-motherfucker walked out the bar and puked. M-m-motherfucker pulled down his pants and pissed." Junior points out the puddles of vomit and urine and you notice that he too has a damaged face and looks to be enormously fatigued and it occurs to you that perhaps the entire neighborhood, this small and unpleasant mini-version of America, is dying all together in a piece. You mention the theory to Junior but he is uninterested. He asks you for twenty dollars and you say no and he turns and walks away. His elbows are scabbed and he is missing a shoe.

YOUR PILFERED-MONIES pile is two and a half feet high and it takes you the length of an episode of *COPS* to count it. Earlier that morning (you now wake up early each morning, without a hangover, feeling glad and clear-headed) you purchased paper money-bands from an office supply store and imagined the cash stacked in crisp and tidy piles as in the heist movies of your youth, but you are disappointed to find that the bills are frayed and crazy and that the stacks resemble kinked hair pushing out from under too tight headbands. At any rate, you have over three thousand dollars. You need more than this but not much more; you want to quit the bar and move on but you cannot, yet; you are anxious to carry on, as you feel that your time at the bar is limited in that you will soon either be fired/imprisoned or "be killed." You do not know how you will "be killed"—there are any number of ways—but one thing is certain: The hearts of the bar are against you, and they do not want you around them any longer.

Discuss Sam, the black cocaine dealer. He dislikes you now. He has his children with him and they do not like you and will not accept your offer of candy or maraschino cherries. Discuss Ignacio, who no longer tells you his impossible-odds penis-adventure stories. Discuss Raymond, who will no longer speak to you and whose rancid coffee breath you have not smelled in several weeks. You have been pushed from their society and you are confused to find yourself hurt in the same way you were hurt in the schoolyard those many years back when the boys took your new ball away and you were forced to play with stones in the dirt and sand. The whiskey continues to sting going down and you notice that the seals on the Jameson bottles are all broken. You realize they are empties that have been filled with well whiskey, the assumed reasons for this being to hurt your feelings, which it does, and to save the bar money, for if an employee is going to steal (as you are suspected of stealing) then there is no reason to furnish him with his drink of choice, when his drink of choice is a fine Irish whiskey. It makes you sad to think of a grown man (you believe it is Simon) funneling this nasty liquor into an empty Jameson bottle and you wonder if he feels happy as he is doing it, or does he also find it sad? A week goes by, two weeks, and he no longer offers to pour you a cupful with a creeping smirk on his face.

You decide you will not drink the well whiskey any longer and now purchase three or four airplane bottles of Jameson on your way to work, sipping these slowly throughout the night in plain view of the regulars, who taunt you, asking how much these cost, and you turn to tell them that it does not matter because after all you are not the one paying for them. Who is paying for them? they ask hopefully. But you are not so angry as to answer the question honestly. "I make my enemies pay," you tell them, and they turn to each other and say, Oooooh.

LANCER RETURNS FROM the cozy abyss of the semi-successful Hollywood actor-writer to visit with his old workmates. This returning to the bar is an important event for him, though you cannot understand why, as he was around for only a few months, and yet when he bounds through the front door he acts as if he is falling in with beloved college chums at a ten-year reunion. He has a collection of people with him who look as though they were manufactured by aliens. He introduces them to you and they claim to have heard all about you, and they smile and beam at you and you do not know exactly why but after a time it becomes clear that Lancer has told them stories relating to your ability to render yourself useless. His dirty-blond hair has been bleached and he is deeply tanned; he is playing the part of a wisecracking swimming pool cleaner in a television pilot, he says. You ask him if he is enjoying himself and he replies by pointing to the breasts of one of his new friends. You ask him if this part he is playing is good or bad and he says that the quality of the piece is irrelevant—he is a working actor in Hollywood and the odds against this happening are so great that he would take the part of a singing shitpile if it kept him out of bars like this one. "But you seem to think it's the greatest thing in the world to be back," you say.

"Only because I don't *have* to be back," he says. "I mean with you I'm sure it's different—you work, you have your wife, you'll probably have kids, right? You're all squared away, but I have dreams, you know? Big dreams. And none of them were going to come true in a place like this."

Lancer says that the airing of his show is fast approaching and asks if you would like to come over to his new house in the hills for the pilot bash and you, imagining how terrible a party at Lancer's house with Lancer's friends and Lancer's musical selections would be, say that you most definitely will not be there and Lancer, who had expected this answer, laughs, and he tells his friend that you are "one of a kind." He turns to you and says with a serious, straight face, "Will you watch it at home, then? Will you watch it at home and root for me?" And though you know you will not you tell him you will, and it means so much to him that your heart breaks a little, and you wish Lancer success in this strange world he has flung himself into and he hugs you and thanks you and when he says goodbye he hands you a hundred-dollar bill, which makes you ashamed, but he says there isn't anything to be ashamed of and you put the money in your pocket and walk him to the door. He and his friends are going to some other more glamorous bar, he tells you, a bar on the Strip, and you mock-retch and he winks and smiles and throws you a mint and is gone. This is the last time you will see Lancer in your lifetime.

You feel the hundred-dollar bill in your front pants pocket and you receive an inspiration, and here is what it is: You walk back into the bar and up to Simon, handing him the money, claiming to have found it on the ground. With all of his suspicions regarding your moral fiber, this is the very last thing he would presently expect you to do, and you can see his mind working, trying to find your angle in this, but at last he decides that there is none—he believes you have found and then turned in one hundred dollars in cash when it would have been the easiest thing in the world to slip the bill into your wallet. At the end of the night, after no one has claimed the money, Simon decides to split it with you, and he says that his faith in you has been restored and you say you are glad. He says that he is sorry for all the things he has been saying about you to the owners and you say, what? He says he will call them in the morning and take them all back and you say, what things? And you are so curious about these secret, evil words that you momentarily forget your stance and open your wallet to tuck away your fifty dollars and Simon sees how much cash you have, and that it has been stashed quickly and haphazardly, and there is no reason for you to have these hundreds of dollars when you have not worked for the past three days and were overheard complaining to a customer earlier about times being tight with your wife gone and the rent resting on your shoulders alone. So Simon, now knowing in his heart that you are a thief, takes the fifty dollars back and puts it in the cash register, and his eyes are swimming in vodka and cocaine and you are worried he will strike you with his cold South African hands but he only turns you toward the door and tells you to go home and get some rest and that you should clear your schedule for the next day because you will be receiving an important telephone call, one that you will not want to miss, but that even if you do miss it, it will not miss you, that is to say: You will be receiving a telephone call that will impart to you news of such consequence that it will transcend its own means of transmission.

Discuss the miracle that visits your life the next day when the phone rings and it is the voice of the owner's wife but she does not fire you or worry you with talk of police and prison as you had been expecting but informs you, through her chokes and sobs, that her husband has died in the nighttime of a massive heart attack. She says there will be a private wake held in three or four days at the bar and that it will be like old times, which you do not understand because which/whose old times is she referring to? She says that each attendee may, if he or she wishes, speak a few words in honor of the deceased, perhaps a fond memory or two, and you say that you will possibly take part but your experiences with the owner were limited and you wonder (to yourself) if you should speak of the time he broke wind in the storage room but did not apologize or even acknowledge it? Or should you discuss the time you caught him picking his nose in his office and you told him to pick a winner and he said that they were all winners? The owner's wife says that she thinks of each employee of the bar as her extended family, and you say, you do? She says that she wants you to know that the owner loved you personally and you say, he did? She says that she knows you loved him too and you do not say any words in response but make a neutral noise, which she luckily does not ask about, and the conversation moves on to practical business matters.

She says she has spoken with Simon about his suspicion that you are a thief, and she asks you what you have to say on the matter. When you do not answer she asks if you have noticed anything strange about Simon's behavior of late, and though you have not you say, yes. She says she has it on good authority that his cocaine intake has recently doubled and you, seeing a light at the end of the tunnel, say tripled, quadrupled, and she sighs and says sadly, I see. She asks about your money-bursting wallet and you invent an excellent on-the-spot lie about your to-be ex-wife paying you cash for divided goods that had been purchased jointly and she, the owner's wife, previously a divorcée, presently a widower, apologizes for bringing it up and blames the talk and suspicions on Simon's obvious stimulant paranoia. You dismiss the apology and tell her you are focused only on her and her grieving family, a lie that she accepts gracefully and as fact and for which she thanks you, though for all the grand statements flying back and forth (her husband *had one life to live,* he *played for keeps, grabbed the bull by the horns, worked hard played hard,* etc.) the owner's wife does not sound all that put out by the death of her mate and in fact by the end of your conversation she is halfheartedly, piteously laughing at the thought of the remainder of her day, to be spent on the telephone, amassing praise and sorrow and condolences, some of it true, some false. She thanks you one last time and says that she will see you at the wake, and that by then she will have the Simon issue straightened out, one way or the other.

WHEN YOU ARRIVE to set up on the night of the wake the bar is empty but you see that a shrine has been put together in honor of the dead owner. The shrine is a foldout table and you look down at the objects resting on top of it, objects meant to conjure fond memories, objects that represent the interests of the deceased: Hamburgers, alcohol, cocaine, and cigarettes. (There is a poster of a palm tree on the wall.) It is a sad collection but you are quick to remind yourself that the contents of your shrine would be similarly unimpressive and you instruct yourself to keep your unkind thoughts at bay. (When the thoughts return you ignore them or try to ignore them.)

Discuss your wife. She calls the bar phone and says that she needs to talk to you about proceeding with the divorce, a word that has the force of a physical object, and you suddenly have no hearing in your ears and though you have long

144

expected this news it paralyzes you, and your wife is concerned by your nonresponse and she calls out your name, frantic and guilt-ridden. In a moment your tongue loosens and you find yourself able to speak and communicate, though your voice is small, your words pathetic and lost-sounding. She begins to cry and then curse you for making her cry, though you are doing nothing other than absorbing the painful information, and she reminds you of all the terrible things you have done and how poorly you treated her when you were together and she says, why couldn't we talk like this before? And you know that it is wrong, your coveting her only after she has left, and that if you were back together you would only return to ignoring her, and you think of what a tricky thing your heart is, and you wonder for the first time if perhaps you have been against yourself all this while?

You say to your wife that she should send whatever awful papers she can come up with to your parents' house. She asks why and you say that you are leaving. She asks where you are going and you say that that is to be decided, and you wish her good luck with her funnyman boyfriend and all his future jokes and she says, hey, wait a minute. You unplug the phone and wrap up the cord and drop it into the trash can.

Simon shows up at nine o'clock, his face red from alcohol. He finds the phone in the trash and without a word removes it, unwraps the cord, and plugs it back into the wall. The bar is still empty and you are alone with him but he will not look at you and you are once again worried that he will strike you down—this is the first time in six years you have seen him arrive at work intoxicated. He drinks one shot after the other and is clearly upset but when you ask him what's the matter he does not answer. Two customers come in and complain about the room's frigid temperature. Simon tells them the bar will host a private party that night, and to leave. After they go

Simon finally turns to you. "She says it's rehab for me or I'm fired, mate."

"Who says?" you say.

"You know who," he says. "And I've got to pay for half. Eight grand."

You do not have any comment for this, search as you might. When he asks what you said to the owner's wife you tell him, "I told her I wasn't stealing. She'd heard you were doing a lot of coke and I said that you were."

Simon nods. You think he is about to cry. Anyway, his lower lip is trembling. "So it's every man for himself," he says.

"It's always been every man for himself."

"Not always," he says. You are surprised by the emotion hovering at the surface of Simon's skin; you are moved when he searches out a fresh bottle of Jameson, real Jameson, which he had hidden some time prior. He breaks the seal and pours you a large shot, a triple, and pours himself one as well, despite the fact that he had been drinking tequila a moment earlier.

"I'm just trying to get out of here," you tell him, by way of apology.

"Never mind," he says. "Here, cheers." And he touches his glass to yours and downs the whiskey in a painful double gulp. You drink yours and you turn to greet the first of the mourners; they enter the bar in a line like postwar soldiers.

DISCUSS THE DRUNKEN WOMAN in the fur coat and smeared lipstick. She is a relative or family friend of the dead owner and she is angry at his passing. You ask if you can take her coat and she is offended and tells you in a slurring monotone, "Keep your hands offa me, Pigeon," which you do, excusing yourself to share another drink with Simon. You and

Simon are now "old and true friends," as though you had dueled with sabers and were both wounded but neither of you killed. He says that he respects you, and you say that you respect him, and he is lying and you are lying. He is very drunk now and Sam the cocaine dealer is late and cannot be reached by telephone. You tell Simon about the small pile resting atop the shrine and he winks at you before lurching away into the back room. The drunken fur-coat woman is demanding service at the end of the bar and you turn to meet her rheumy eyes and she says, "Come on, Pidge, lady wants service down here." You approach her; her fists are rapping the bar and her hair is in her eyes and you cannot help but smile at her getup and outlook. "Speshalty of the house?" she says. You tell her there is a two-for-one deal on nonalcoholic beer with a one-round limit per customer and she nods her head and points at you, turning to share her dislike with someone beside her (but there is no one beside her). "Funny fucker," she says. "You're a real funny little fucker, aren't you? Now I'm going to ask you 'gain, Pidge. What's the speshalty? Of the house? You understand me?" And you, deciding you will ruin this terrible woman's night, say to her casually, "Long Island iced teas are nice."

"What?" she says. "Tea? I don't want any tea. I want a drink!"

You assure her it is a drink, and she asks if it is a strong one. When you say that it is she asks for two, and you go ahead and mix them into pint glasses: Well vodka, well tequila, well rum, well gin, triple sec, sweet and sour, topped with cola. She opens her mouth wide to locate the straw and takes a long sip, smacking her lips and nodding her approval. "Say, that's pretty good, Pigeon," she says. She finishes the glass in three minutes and takes up the second and staggers into the back room, nearly full now with the mourners.

The owner's wife comes up and asks that you have a drink with her, and you do. She is dressed in black and is approached by one mourner after the other; they tell her how sorry they are and remind her how special her husband was and that life is a tragedy for the living and dead both. She sighs and asks you to have another drink with her but you are out of practice and your head is beginning to swim and it is only ten-thirty and so you decline and she drinks alone. Simon has now ceased working and you and the owner's wife watch him through the doorway. He is telling a loud, would-be comical story but nobody is paying him any mind and he, realizing this, sidles up to the shrine with a cautious glance over both shoulders. You try to steal away the attention of the owner's wife but she will not be moved and she watches as Simon licks his pinkie, dips into the little pile of cocaine, and numbs his gums. She turns to you and says, "I can't believe I spent the day feeling guilty about sending that shithead to rehab." She asks for another drink and you make her one. You ask her if there will be any exceptions made to the no-complimentary-drink policy, pointing out that several people have taken offense to the idea that money will be made at a wake, and she shrugs and says that she doesn't care, and to give it all away, if only for a night. She leans in and tells you that she is going home, and you hold your hand out to shake it and she pulls you in to kiss your cheek. She leaves by the side door, smiling at you as she goes, and you wonder at her perfume and the lack of feelings in her heart for her dead husband. She looked beautiful in her mourning dress, you decide.

Simon is singing an eighties pop song in the back room. Someone calls for quiet and Simon shouts out, "Fuck it!" and it occurs to you that you will be in charge for the night, a fact that begets a special and uncommon plan in your mind, a plan to end all plans in fact, and you move quickly to the men's room and force yourself to vomit and afterward pour yourself a cola and slap your own face to wake your brain so as to see this plan through with a minimum of error. *"Now,"* you say to the crowd of heads and bodies. They have filled the bar to capacity and are lining up at the door and calling out for drinks, sympathy, drinks, cigarettes, drinks.

YOU DO NOT HAND OUT free drinks but charge full price, claiming it to be the will of the widow, and also you tell the mourners that the credit card machine is malfunctioning and so it is a cash-only bar. There is some outcry over this, as it is a private party and surely the deceased would have wished it otherwise, but you claim to those complaining that the widow is beside herself with grief and that her instructions were explicit and that she said to you that your job was on the line over the matter, and you tell the mourners that you are sorry but your hands are tied, and you hold up your hands for emphasis, and they reach for their wallets and are angry but their anger is not for you or not for you only.

You place a Post-it over the cash register display which reads, *Should Auld Acquaintance Be Forgot, and Quickly.* You never liked the owner, not his Mercedes, not his scaly bald spot, not the way he slapped your back with his stinging, heavily ringed hand when he greeted you. You are glad he died; you hope that the bar dies along with him and you are visited by the fantasy that you will go and see the widow and woo her and, once you have gained admission to her heart, you will with great seriousness and determination spend every penny she has in her widow's safe of lonely, bloody, loser money. (The Post-it elicits some questioning comments but surprisingly little in the way of anger or hostility.)

Simon, suffering from proletarian guilt, has returned to work but cannot work efficiently and only gets in your way. Sam is still missing and what little cocaine Simon could glean by dipping his pinkie into the dead owner's pile has not taken his edge off, or put his edge on, or whichever it is, and he is trying to act as though this is just another night of work but he cannot shake the shaker without it slipping from his hand and he cannot understand why the credit card machine is not working (you unplugged it earlier) and he cannot fathom and in fact seems a little frightened by this cryptic note covering the register display and all is stuttering, bumbling mess. Finally he turns to you and asks what the hell is going on tonight, and is it just him or does everything seem to be off and unfriendly and wrong? You tell him that you alone will handle this crowd and that his job should be either to go home and vomit into his pillowcase or else to monitor the happenings of the wake and maintain order, and you point to the back room where the mourners are growing drunker and louder and stupider but Simon, looking into the darkness of the room, says to you, "What do I care about them?" And then to himself, "Eight fucking grand." His feelings are hurting just as yours have been hurting and you think you should reach out to him emotionally, for you and Simon are merely pawns in this desperate game of profitable late-night liver abuse/suicide, but when you tap Simon's arm to talk about this he tilts his chin away (to display his handsome jaw line) and says he will not vomit into his pillowcase, will not vomit at all, and that he is sick of what he calls your "weird-word bullshit," and he combs his hair in the mirror over the bar and struts into the back room and you watch with a mixture of respect and pity as he falls to his knees and frankly inhales the dead man's cocaine pile. The back room falls silent over this, and you see a moment later that Simon is joined on both sides by two squirming bodies, also on their knees, scrambling to collect some of this pile for themselves—it is Curtis and the child actor, and the scene is so vivid to you, so vivid and gripping and horrific that you wave away drink orders and shush a nearby group of vocal mourners so that you can concentrate on the happenings with all your might and interest.

Y OU WANT TERRIBLY to drink and one customer after another offers to buy you a round but you resist because, one, you must keep track of your fast-growing pilfered monies and, two, you want to be able to recall this night, which you suddenly realize will be your last here. The Teachers are at the bar, talking about the incident with the cocaine pile. They are disgusted and you hear one of them say, in a surprisingly grand statement, that death has devolved toward meaninglessness.

"What kind of an asshole puts coke on his shrine, anyway?" she wonders.

"Really," says the other. And then, "Course, that wasn't him, though."

"No," agrees the first. "But you know what I mean."

Simon, Curtis, and the child actor are sitting at the bar talking about you, gesturing toward you, staring at you. None of them are smiling and they have obviously been speaking about how much they have recently come to dislike you, and Simon has told his story about your telling the dead owner's wife about his cocaine intake and now you can overhear them calling you a rat and a dog, and you walk over and say, three little bears, three little pigs, to which they make no response. They are, you suppose, hoping to intimidate you. They are brooding, and you wonder if the cocaine from the shrine was heavily cut or entirely counterfeit, as they seem merely drunk. They are talking about this same thing: "You feel it?" Curtis asks. "I don't feel it. Do you feel it?" asks the child actor. Simon is dead drunk and totally confused, and you once more tell him to go home and vomit and be sick throughout the night and the next day. "Get it over with," you say. "These two aren't going to help you any."

"Like you helped me?" he says.

"Yeah," says the child actor.

"Yeah," says Curtis.

"Yeah," you say, giving up, because what do you care if these three do not like you? But as you turn away you realize with a shame-jolt that you do care. But what reason is there to care? You just do. You don't want to like them; you can't like them—they are unlikable—but you want them to like you or to pretend to like you, as before. It is some kind of diseased, anti-moral conditioning, you decide.

You walk down the bar and find the woman in the fur coat, an empty pint glass in her hand. One of her eyes is closed and she is shrugging and talking to Junior the crack addict, who has never to your knowledge been admitted into the bar and whose hulking presence is completely incongruous, up-setting your sense of aesthetics—something like discovering a rooster in a town car. Junior looks up at you and his face is scabbed and he is picking at it. He peels away a large scab and his wound is exposed and moist. His eyes are vibrating from bad drugs and he does not seem to recognize you. He is taller than those standing near him though he is sitting down. "My man," he says, snapping his fingers. "Seven and s-seven over here. Give the lady w-whatever she wants."

"Junior, how did you get in here?" you ask.

"I just came right in," he says, and his bloated fingers

mimic a man walking. He holds out a wad of one-dollar bills. "What's a matter, my money ain't g-g-g-g-g-g-g-green?"

"'Nother tea," says the woman in the fur coat.

You go outside for a cigarette and see that Brent is not at the door and that his car is gone. People are streaming into the bar now and there is very little room to move inside. People are screaming and slapping the bar for service. Mourners are crying openly on the sidewalk, their faces wet beneath the streetlights. You will never find out the reason for Brent's departure or where he has gone; you will never see him again in your life. You are turning to reenter the bar when you notice a body lying splayed on the sidewalk across the street, in front of the terrible building that vomits humans, a sight that makes the small cuts on your hands throb. Your chin instantly trembles and you begin to tell the mourners that there has been another suicide when the body shivers and stands and walks away, though for some reason you are not relieved by this, only confused and lost-feeling. Your hands are throbbing doubly now and you look at them, at the little cuts on your palms and finger pads, and you think of the game you used to play, counting these wounds and cuts in the sink water. Why did you stop playing this game? And what was the word the ghost woman used, the word you did not know but that she put in your mind for you to look up in the dictionary? And what happened to the ghost woman, where did she go? Were ghosts led away when it was time or did they simply *know* and go on their own?

"'Nother iced tea," the drunk woman repeats when you return.

"Seven and s-seven, my man," says Junior.

You make them their drinks and Junior gives you his money, asking for the remainder in change, only there is no remainder and he is in fact seven dollars short, which you forgive him, but he is outraged at the cost of liquor and he protests when you tell him that the fur coat woman's drink alone was ten dollars.

"For tea?" he says. "Ten dollars for a glass of tea?"

The fur coat woman smacks her lips. "Worth ever' penny," she says. "I'm a changed woman, Pidge. Gonna be iced tea from here on out."

But Junior will never forgive you. "Ten dollars," he says, shaking his head. He leads the fur coat woman into the back room, ducking to get under the doorway. You are preparing drinks when you see in the mirror that Ignacio has joined Simon and the others. He pulls out a flick knife and stabs in the direction of your back and the group laughs. You turn around and he secretes the knife up his sleeve and watches you contemptibly. "What the fuck are you looking at?" he asks.

"Out-and-out hostility," you say to him/them.

"So?" he asks, his arm hanging protectively over Simon's shoulder.

You lean in. Your feelings are truly, deeply hurt. "To think I humored you for such a long, long time," you say to him. And for a split second there is actual human emotion shuttling between the two of you, and you see that he partially regrets his going along with the group decision to ostracize you. But then he regains his footing and returns to his animosity. "Back up," he says sharply, waving his hand in your face. "Go tell it to someone who cares." Excellent advice, you think, and you look around the room for this person and when you do not find him/her you decide it is time to leave the bar and never return. But you cannot leave without packing your pilfered monies and you cannot pack your pilfered monies with these four sitting at the bar watching you. Now Raymond joins their ranks, pulling a pile of napkins toward himself. He plucks a pen from his ART SAVES LIVES T-shirt and begins to draw, occasionally looking up at you as though searching for hateful inspiration.

A marvelous inspiration: You act as if the phone is ringing and you rush to pick it up. You turn and watch these five ghouls with a look of growing concern on your face. You cover your ear as though the music and bar noise are upsetting your conversation but you call out, loud enough to be heard, "Now? You're coming in now? No, Simon's in the bathroom. Drunk? No, he's had a couple. Not drunk, though. I'll tell him you're coming. All right. I'll tell him. Yes. Goodbye." You hang up and see the group is watching you intently and you move over to them and share your invented news, which is that the owner's wife has heard that Simon is too drunk to work, and she is mortally offended he picked the night of her husband's wake to disregard his duties. She is on her way, you tell them, and if she finds him any more drunk than usual—that is, too drunk to work—she will revoke her offer of a partially paid rehabilitation with his position intact upon discharge and simply fire him outright. Now the group is confused about what they should do next. Simon is talking and you are all listening to him and it sounds as though he thinks it best that he "face the music," but after asking him to repeat his syrupy words you realize he is saying, "What's this music?" He says that it reminds him of a special girl, a long-gone girl, a girl who stole his heart, and he starts describing her physically ("Tits right outta *National Geographic*") when Sam the cocaine dealer walks up and is verbally brutalized for his tardiness at so crucial a juncture as this. By way of explanation Sam says that he is slow-moving for two reasons, namely his mourning the death of the owner, his old friend, and also because of some mystery-violence, and he points to a cut on his face, a small, deep puncture just below his eye, which does not issue blood but looks grotesque and painful. It is a long and vicious story, he says, and would anyone like to hear it?

However, there is no time to lose, or rather there is, but you must pretend there is not, and you hustle the group to the privacy of the back office, and as they are settling Simon onto the leather couch you take Sam aside and tell him the story about the owner's wife and the looming threat of Simon's unemployment. When you are finished you ask him if he can straighten Simon out and he says of course he can, but only for a fee. You instruct Curtis and the child actor to rifle Simon's pants and they do, discovering his wallet, which is empty; you instruct everyone to chip in for Simon's pick-me-up but nobody moves. "I only have enough for myself," says the child actor. "I don't even have that much," Curtis says. "I was going to take some of his." Finally you inform the group that if Simon is fired (the owner's wife is on her way, you say again), they will all be forced to pay full price for their drinks forever, news that brings forth the necessary cash, and in a moment Simon is being propped up on the couch and a mirror full of cocaine is placed below his pasty pink face. You tell him he will soon be all right and he looks up at you and smiles, or nearly smiles, or possibly sneers, and you wonder if this will be the last time you ever see him; you hope it is but at the same time you experience a feeling like friendliness tinged with remorse. "Goodbye," you say to him, and to the group. They say nothing. You turn and go.

You return to the bar and take up the pilfered monies in a bank bag—the overfull bag will not zip closed and you wrap it in a dishrag. The mourners are frantic for drinks and have begun throwing napkins at you and calling you unkind and vulgar names; when they see that you have returned only to leave once more, the largest man in the crowd stops you by placing his fist on your chest, and he spins you around and orders you to go back to work. He is drunk and wants badly to strike you down; you turn to tell him there is an old man having a seizure in the parking lot and that he will die if you do not bring him his medicine, and you hold up your coat, claiming it is the old man's. Now this enormous drunk becomes heroic, and in a flash he is pushing the customers roughly out of your way to clear a path, shouting, "Move it! We're trying to save a life here!" He shuttles you past the screaming masses and as you enter the back room he slaps your shoulders and wishes you luck and Godspeed. You thank him and tell him to help himself to the beer cooler while you are away and he says that he absolutely will, and he rushes off to do just that.

There is a twenty-person line for the bathroom but you need desperately to urinate and you cut to the front, claiming an employee emergency, and you suffer the many jeers and boos of the impatient crowd. The man at the head of the line is in a rage, and he says that "they" have been in the lone stall for fifteen minutes and you pull yourself up on the stall door to peer over and you are surprised to see that the fur coat woman is fellating Junior, or had been fellating Junior, as she seems to have fallen asleep mid-task. Junior is delicately slapping her face. "Focus, baby, focus," he says. She opens her eyes and goes back to work automatically. The size of Junior's erect organ is preposterous. It is enough to blind your eyes. It is, you say to yourself, impossible.

"How are you not famous?" you ask him, and he looks up at you.

"Papa was a rollin' stone," he sings, though you are not sure if this is his answer or if his mind is elsewhere. There is blood running down his face. This is the last time you will see Junior, and you wave goodbye.

You are urinating in the sink. The man at the head of the line is watching you; he has blown his own mind with anger and frustration. He is hitting the wall and you wonder if he will hit you, but he does not, though he wants to and claims that you deserve to be hit, which you suppose is probably true and you agree with the man that it is true. You zip up and walk past him and he spits on you and you feel the spit hit your back. The people in the line like this and they applaud and congratulate the spitting man, and you look back and see his glad, bashful face, and you watch him accepting the handshakes and awkward high-fives of his neighbors, and he is so proud to have spit on you and you are certain that this has been the highlight of his day and night and the sight of his fat, glad face seizes your throat and you sob, and you will sob more if you do not pay close attention and contain your emotions, which you do, but you wonder why this man's meaningless life and face aroused such a feeling in you, a feeling that should, at some point, be discussed. You unwrap the dishrag from the bank bag and use it to wipe the spit from your back. You drop the rag to the ground and spit on it.

You enter the back room headlong, the bank bag tucked close to your side. Instantly you are aware that something has happened here since your trip to the bathroom, some type of upset, for the people around you are motionless, their eyes all directed at a fixed point in the room's center. You follow their eyes and see that the shrine has been toppled and that there are two groups of men, the previously-warring and the to-be-warring; some of them are bleeding from their faces and you, folding your arms to watch one last act of depravity, say it aloud to the man standing next to you: "Perfect."

Discuss the two previously- and to-be-warring parties. On one side are the brothers and uncles of the deceased. They look like members of the Mafia or anyway what members of the Mafia look like on television and in movies: Large, imposing, masculine, unshaven or lazily shaven, and out of shape.

Opposite this group are Simon, Curtis, the child actor, Raymond, Sam, and Ignacio. Ignacio is at the front of the pack and
he has his knife out; he is slashing at his impenetrable pants
with the blade and saying, "See? You see that? Cocksuckers!"
Apparently he is hoping to show that he cannot be hurt or that
it will be difficult to hurt him—his eyes are larger, uglier, and
crazier than you have ever seen them and you realize that his
many stories of violence and retribution were probably half
true. But why, you wonder, are these groups at war? You ask
a woman at your side and she says, "Those big guys caught
the blond bartender eating a hamburger from the table. One
of them hit him and then they all went nuts." You look at Simon; he has some remnant of the sandwich clutched in his
fist and there is mustard smeared on his cheek, mingling with
the blood trickling from his nostrils. He is shivering and has
clearly done his fair share of Sam's cocaine but not enough to
straighten himself out entirely. He is straddling two worlds,
lost somewhere between being overly drunk and overly high,
and he does not understand what is happening and you have
an urge to help him because you can see that there will soon
be more violence and that the bar crew is at a disadvantage in
both the size and the sobriety department. Finally you call out
to him, beckoning with your hand, and he locates you in the
crowd and smiles and waves. Then he looks down and sees
the bank bag under your arm, and you suppose he does not
understand the precise reason you might be holding such a
thing but he does know in his heart that it is incorrect and he
makes a move toward you, saying, "Wait. No. Wait a minute.
Stop." You back up, looking for an exit, wondering if you will
have to fight to remove yourself, but then you see that this will
not be necessary because Simon has walked directly into the
group of men he was only a minute earlier warring with and
they, believing that he is making a hostile advance, knock him

to the ground, sending the halved hamburger flying through the air, and the two groups now dog-pile each other, clumsy hands swinging in the smoky semi-darkness.

The crowd pushes in to catch a sharper glimpse of the slaughter, and as the room constricts you sneak away to the luxurious silence of the magical Ford. Your hands and shoulders are shaking from nerves and fatigue but you have the presence of mind to hide the bank bag deep beneath the passenger seat before entering traffic. You drive slowly home; the side streets are empty, the anonymous smaller roads of the slumbering working class. You do not see any policemen and you pat the seat beside you in thanks. You leave the Ford idling in the carport and bound up the stairs to pack a suitcase before writing a note to the landlords with instructions to sell your furniture and enjoy the deposit. You gather your previously and newly pilfered monies together in a pillowcase and return to the Ford to make your lifetime getaway but you discover that this last trip home has used up the car's magic entirely; the engine has seized and will not turn over. You sit in the carport, exhausted, staring at and feeling amazed by the utterly dead dashboard. You return to your house and call a taxi service; the dispatcher says a cab will be there in fifteen to twenty minutes and you thank her and unplug the telephone and place it in the trash can. You return to the Ford to wait. The crickets have ceased chirping. It is that unknown and otherworldly chasm that exists between the nighttime and the day.

THE POCKMARKED COUNTER MAN is kicking the bottoms of your feet and telling you to wake up. "Wake up," he says. It is seven o'clock in the morning and your face is slick with dew and sweat.

"What?" you say. "What?"

"I'm calling the cops."

"I'm awake, I'm awake," you say, standing up too quickly and nearly fainting. You sit back down. You were asleep atop your pillowcase of money. Your suitcase is at your side. You are in front of the car rental agency.

The taxi driver who brought you here, an African immigrant with deeply black skin and worried yellow eyes, had been curious about you and asked you some questions so as to understand your place in the world.

"But the agency does not open for several hours," he had said.

"That's all right," you told him. "Distance from the scene of the crime is what's important now."

"Scene of the crime," he repeated. His eyes flashed at you in the rear-view mirror.

"I tipped poorly though I knew it was wrong," you explained. "I spoke closely and with bad breath. I drank recklessly, without remorse. I spoke excessively about myself with no regard for truth or the boredom of others." You scratched your face and nodded, agreeing with yourself. "I slept badly but I've lived to tell the tale."

"You are making a joke I think," said the taxi driver.

"I don't know."

"You are unhappy?"

"I have been unhappy," you told him.

"But now is vacation time?" he said hopefully.

"You're a nice man," you said, and he shrugged.

The pockmarked counter man is not so nice, and worse, he remembers you from the last time you were here. His outlook, which was previously poor, seems to have worsened and so you can only assume that his life has worsened. It is sad to think of the daily workings of this ugly, unhappy man, and your head is hurting but you have no aspirin to ease your pain. You ask the counter man for aspirin and he says he has none; somehow you know he is lying to you. So here is the final trial, the renting of a vehicle from a man who does not like you and who will never like you, but whom you must deal with in an efficient manner lest you remain without transportation, which would allow you the freedom to roam and escape, but to where you have not yet decided.

"What's the quickest route out of California?" you ask.

"What?" he asks, tapping the keys of his keyboard. "What?"

"I want a fast car this time," you say. "Forget about the legroom. I want the fastest, most dangerous car you've got on the lot."

The man leans over and sniffs forthrightly. He asks that you prepare yourself a cup of complimentary coffee, which he has just brewed, and you do, and it tastes terrible. You stand near the brochure display and listen in on the counter man's telephone conversation. He is speaking once more with his regional manager, and once more he is hoping to render you carless, and he speaks of your unpleasant odor and your desire to escape the state of California, and once more the regional manager sides with you, and you understand through the comments made by the counter man that his boss is similarly disinclined toward the Golden State: "Smog, I know, sir. Traffic, yes. Yes, the pollution. Yes, I understand, sir. But this *guy* . . ."

It is no use, and the counter man is forced to rent you the car. By the end of your transaction the man is slamming down pens and handling the paperwork with unconcealed malice and you watch him going hatefully through the motions and you feel a distinct pity and sadness for this man, and just after he hands you the key to your new sports car, which you plan to demolish through misuse and overuse, you say to him, "It's none of my business, but I think it might be time for you to switch professions."

The man's face is cold and thoughtless. "It's none of your business," he agrees.

"It's none of my business," you say, "but I think it might be time for you to quit working altogether."

"Quit working and do what?"

"Try to be happy?" you say.

The man is looking into your eyes. You hoped to offer him an alternative to his present, obviously unsatisfactory lifestyle but your words sounded silly and childish, and though you had his attention for a moment you have now lost it and he returns to tap at his keyboard, shaking his head at your foolishness.

"Thank you," you say, and as you walk to the door, to your sports car waiting at the curb, the tapping of the keys trails off and you believe he is watching you and thinking about you and wondering about what you have said to him. And as you drive away from Los Angeles you think of this man tapping and worrying and hating, and you think of the kindhearted taxi driver and all of his probable problems and backaches and heartaches, and you think of Simon, presently unconscious on the putrid carpeted floor of the bar, his face dirtied with ashes and blood and mustard, and you think of yourself and of the six years you spent with your skeleton arms shivering in the cold brown water of the bar sinks and you are repulsed with yourself for allowing your unhappiness to continue for so long a time, and you promise yourself that you will never be stuck in such a position as this again, that you will try to be happy, as you said to the counter man, childish or silly or otherwise, it makes no difference. I will try to be happy, you think, and your heart and chest feel a plummeting, as in the case of the hurtling rollercoaster, and your heart wants to cry and sob, but you, not wanting to cry, hit yourself hard in the center of your chest and it hurts so much but you drive on, your face dry and remaining dry, though it had been a close call, after all.

Time passes and you shake your head. "Work will drive you crazy if you let it," you say. You do not speak for a long time after this.

# Acknowledgments

Leslie Napoles

Gustavo Valentine deWitt
Susan deWitt
Mike deWitt
Nick deWitt

Peter McGuigan
Hannah Gordon Brown
Stephanie Abou
Foundry Literary

Jenna Johnson
Tina Pohlman
Laurence Cooper

Dennis Cooper
Matt Sweeney
D. V. DeVincentis
Hunter Kennedy
Andy Hunter
Carson Mell
Azazel Jacobs

Gabriel Liebeskind